Fire And Ice

Copyright © 2003 William Graham
All rights reserved.
No part of this book may be reproduced, stored in a retrieval system,
or transmitted by any means, electronic, mechanical, photocopying,
recording, or otherwise, without written permission from the author.

ISBN: 1-58898-913-5

WILLIAM GRAHAM

FIRE AND ICE

A NOVEL

2003

Fire And Ice

To Jacqueline

Some say the world will end in fire,
Some say in ice.
From what I've tasted of desire
I hold with those who favor fire.
But if I had to perish twice,
I think I know enough of hate
To say that for destruction ice
Is also great
And would suffice.

"Fire and Ice"—Robert Frost

CHAPTER 1

Christa Bennington put her two-and-a-half year old daughter Paris to bed in what was once her old bedroom in the house on Bluff Street. She was reared in Lacroix. An old town of large brick houses, porches and long memories, Lacroix was perched on the gentle hills overlooking the Mississippi River. Lacroix was far removed from the glamorous life Christa once lived in Chicago and New York. But Lacroix was where she was born forty-two years ago.

She returned to Lacroix four years ago when her mother Eva was diagnosed with cancer. An only child, Christa felt obligated to return to Lacroix and comfort her mother—a widow for over ten years. A sense of obligation and exhaustion pushed Christa back to Lacroix. Obligation to her mother to whom she had drawn closer as she became more unfulfilled with her career. After nearly twenty years in the advertising industry, corporate mergers and takeovers had sapped her of the feelings of enjoyment and accomplishment that had fueled her rise in her profession and in the New York social scene.

While immersed in the advertising world and climbing to the chief executive's suite at Franklin Worldwide, Christa seldom returned to Lacroix. After heading off to attend Smith College, she never wanted to return to what she called the smothering provincialism of her hometown. But when she reached her late thirties, what she was thought was smothering was now comforting and what had been provincial turned magically into peaceful familiarity.

Her childhood home was a symbol of stability and comfort—from the creaking wood floors to the sound of the washer and dryer reverberating against the concrete basement walls to the large oak trees in the ample backyard providing shade in the summer and a crunching carpet of leaves in the autumn. She had persuaded her mother, however, to update the house's kitchen and bathroom with contemporary plumbing and cabinets and new floors. Although she wrapped herself in childhood memories of the cavernous old house, she also wanted to live in a house that worked and met the standards that she had set in New York.

The oak tree was now bare and covered with frozen snow. Two days earlier, a bitter winter storm had deposited over a foot of snow, which was followed by a sarcastic snap of below zero temperatures. Christa looked out at the frozen landscape and thought that the fresh flowers she had just placed on her mother's grave were now buried in snow. She thought to herself as she sipped her cup of tea that there was nothing more bleak than a graveyard in winter. "In the bleak midwinter," she murmured as she descended the staircase from her daughter's room to the den, where she went to read before going to bed.

The combination of the hot tea and the warm blanket she wrapped around her shoulders made her sleepy. She didn't know how long the doorbell had been ringing before she heard it. She was afraid that the sound would wake Paris up. She walked briskly to the door and opened it. "What do you want?" she barked at the person standing on the porch.

She could feel the cold air biting through her slippers and her hot blood rushing to her face like lava. She rushed the person in just as an uninvited gust of cold wind whipped through the door and rattled the blinds on the windows.

CHAPTER 2

Across town on Hampton Court, a new subdivision where each house had a cathedral ceiling in the livingroom and a large deck thrusting out over a sloping backyard like the bow of a ship, Nora Morrissey reclined in her bed watching a home decorating show on cable. She was addicted to programs that featured well-groomed hosts with soft, reassuring voices discussing the details of renovated houses that had been transformed from the drab and commonplace into something elegant, stylish or whimsical.

She thought that her new house was drab and commonplace, but at least it was spacious, offering plenty of room for her and her husband Randy and their two daughters: twelve-year-old Alexandra and ten-year-old Jenna. She had wanted a French country decorating theme with plenty of blues and yellows throughout the house, however. She loved the rustic elegance and simplicity of French farmhouses. She had dreamed of traveling to France and returning with an album of photos that would become the inspiration for her dream house. But she had never traveled to France, except vicariously through magazines and television shows. Even if she could visit the type of house she had desired, she knew that Randy would never approve, for he wanted everything to be clean and sleek and modern, like all of the other houses on Hampton Court.

Nora often dreamed of the smells of fresh fabric and new wood and flowers. These smells were a comforting contrast to the aromas that she usually encountered on her job: sweat, urine, beer-stained walls and the gasoline smell of a bad car accident. Nora Morrissey was a detective with the Lacroix Police Department. She had followed in the large footsteps of her father, the former Lacroix Police Chief Earl Lamereaux.

Her father had never wanted her to pursue a career in law enforcement, even in a quiet town like Lacroix. But Nora couldn't be discouraged by her father or her mother Marie, whom she knew prayed for her safety every morning at St. Patrick's church.

Nora wanted to chart her own life and career. She had defined independence as having a fulfilling career and being able to travel beyond the borders of the midwest. That was before she met Randy Morrissey, who had inherited Morrissey Motors from his father. Electric passion led quickly to cool commitment. Nora soon found herself walking down the aisle with one of the richest men in Lacroix. She dreamed that she and Randy would travel the world together. But during their marriage Randy became entangled in his business and announced that he had never been that interested in foreign travel anyway.

So Nora gave up her dreams of travel to foreign lands, but she had refused to quit the police force, in spite of Randy's protestations. When she announced that she had been promoted to detective, she was met with a lukewarm hug and kiss on the cheek by Randy, who then headed to the den to watch Sports Center on ESPN.

Randy was in the den once again, probably watching Australian-rules football or a cricket match, Nora thought. If the sport had a ball in it, Randy would watch it, Nora told her friends and colleagues. Nora clicked off the television. Randy had been coming to bed later and later, sometimes not until two or three o'clock in the morning. He told her that he needed to clear his mind from the stress of the long day. Nora had stopped questioning his behavior. It was Randy's income as the leading retailer of Nissans and Subarus in the tri-state area that had provided this house for her and the girls. Nora's salary as a detective in Lacroix was paltry in comparison. But her job and her paycheck still made her proud. She turned up the heat on the second floor of the house and then buried herself under her comforter. She hated the cold.

CHAPTER 3

Declan O'Brien put on a CD of Duke Ellington's *Latin American Suite*. Ellington's jazzy beats and Latin-flavored solos warmed the room as much as the fire burning in the fireplace. Declan sat quietly in his chair, letting the music soak into him so that he could picture the hot sands of Acapulco and the riotous carnival in Rio. Such visions were a welcome distraction from the frost-covered windows and the sarcastic winter wind that whipped around his house on Devereaux Street in Lacroix.

Declan's house was a block away from St. Francis College, where his father Gerald had taught English for over forty years. Declan used to joke with his friends that his father was indeed a walking cliché of an English professor—tweed jacket, beaten up briefcase and possessing the musty smell of an old library. His father never had lofty scholarly aspirations. Although he did publish a few articles and an obscure book on Hamlin Garland, Gerald O'Brien was content to teach writing and American literature to vaguely interested students year after year. He considered it his calling to at least make successive generations aware that there was a language of "truth and beauty" that was as important as the more dominant lexicon of commerce and popular culture. "I fight the good fight," he often told Declan.

His father used to read quietly and grade papers in the same room in which Declan now sat. Now it was Declan's house, Declan's study, Declan's chair. He had been back in Lacroix for four months, working as the city desk editor of the *Lacroix Herald*. His high school friend Thomas McCallum—who was the paper's publisher-- had offered him the job, rescuing Declan from a real estate journal that was published by a Chicago-based trade association.

After fifteen years away from Lacroix going to school and living in Chicago, Declan had returned to Lacroix. Returned for good after coming back to bury his parents who had died in a traffic accident in the summer.

This was one of those evenings when Declan could not reconcile himself to the seismic shift in circumstances that had deposited him back along the banks of the Mississippi River. So he let his mind drift off to thoughts of a Mexican hacienda as a delicate saxophone solo hung in the air like a lover's whisper.

He wondered what his ex-wife Kate was doing now. She had managed their house in a Chicago suburb. That seemed fair to Declan because her parents had bought it for them. She also handled a large portion of his retirement account. She grew up with money and liked to handle it. Declan gladly deferred to her on monetary matters.

Declan surmised that she was probably at a trendy restaurant in the city or watching the BBC news or *Brideshead Revisited* for the tenth time on television. He knew that Kate could never stand just to sit and listen to good music and daydream. After a few years of marriage, Kate realized that Declan was not a driven man, at least not driven to corporate success. Kate had visions of Declan being publisher of the *Chicago Tribune* before he turned thirty-five. Declan just loved to write and report on what he saw. Their mutual love of travel even began to diverge. Kate wanted to go to the French Riviera. Declan wanted to go on safaris or hiking in Alaska. Their marriage ended without much bitterness or acrimony, more like two drivers who exchange insurance information after a minor car accident. But if he had a few too many drinks, Declan would bitterly refer to Kate as that "blond woman who had a price tag on her head."

He had not been outside all day. It was one of those punishing Midwestern winter days when the moment you step outside the hairs in your nose freeze and the tips of your ears start burning and then become red and numb. Declan could never believe that anyone truly got used to such a climate even if they bravely said they did.

FIRE AND ICE

Declan put another log on the fire and settled back into his chair, reopening the pages of Raymond Chandler's *The Long Goodbye*. He nursed a glass of port and scratched his brown hair, which was beginning to turn gray near his temples. He held the book away from his face so that he could see the words through his glasses. He refused to purchase reading glasses. He did not want to surrender yet to old age before he was forty years old.

His cat Melville snoozed near the warmth of the fireplace. Even though Declan was surrounded by the volumes of literature that his father had collected through the decades, he wasn't going to spend the evening trying to mine the meaning in the poems of Emily Dickinson or the novels of Hawthorne. He had too many conversations of this type with his father when he was growing up. He didn't want to remember things like that now. That would be just too brutal. It was better to read about men who drank took much booze and hung around with the wrong type of broads in Los Angeles.

As he read, Declan's head became heavy and it fell on his chest. Ellington's dreamy Latin concoctions had put him to sleep. He suddenly awoke to sounds of sirens that drifted through the still winter night. Melville opened his eyes when Declan did, but he decided that it wasn't worth the effort to investigate the noise any further. Melville yawned once and then closed his eyes again.

Declan looked out of the window toward the west and saw a fire burning in the distance. He pressed his nose against the frigid window and stared at the flames piercing the sky a few miles away. Declan figured that the fire was outside of the city where there were still many family farms. It might be a barn fire, he thought. His watch read eleven o'clock.

He called the newspaper's office and reached Phil Haslett, who had heard about the fire on the police scanner. Twice divorced, Phil had been with the newspaper for over twenty years, never rising above the rank of city reporter. That was fine with Phil, Declan had discovered. Phil had low expectations but performed his job with predictability if not enthusiasm or inspiration.

He told Declan that he was on his way to the scene and that he would have the story ready for Declan in the morning. He knew that Phil lived for opportunities like this—fires, auto accidents, domestic batteries in the middle of the night. If such events didn't occur occasionally, Declan thought as he turned off the CD player, Phil would spend yet another lonely evening in an empty newsroom looking at pornographic web sites. Even though it was bitter cold tonight, Phil would be forced to deal with some reality rather than sexual fantasy. Strangely comforted by that thought, Declan climbed the stairs to his bedroom and retired for the evening. He knew that Melville would follow him after the heat from the fireplace had died out.

CHAPTER 4

The red digital numbers on her bedroom clock read one o'clock when the phone rang at the Morrissey home. Nora was awakened from what she called "the sleep of the dead." She sat up and saw that Randy had finally come to bed after his evening gorging of sports. She didn't know how long the phone had been ringing before she picked it up.

"Hello," she said wearily. She thought that it might be the mysterious fax machine sound that often screeched in her ear in the middle of the night. But it wasn't. It was a sound of a voice that she was trying to recognize.

"Nora, it's Dave," the voice said.

"Dave? Dave who?"

"Dave Henderson. Come on, Nora, no kidding around. Officer Henderson. You need to get out here to the Reynolds place on Route 14 as soon as possible."

"Dave, I'm sorry. I'm still sleepy," Nora said, sitting up in bed and trying to regain consciousness and some semblance of rational thought. "What was that again?"

"We need you here at the Reynolds place on Route 14. There's been a fire."

"A fire? Why do you need me at a fire scene anyway? That's the fire department's job."

"Not when there are two dead bodies in the rubble," Dave said.

"I'm still not following you. Did they die in the fire? You're taking about the owners—the Reynolds."

"That's why we need you here, Nora. Judd and Miriam Reynolds were found shot. How soon can you get here?"

"Jesus Christ," Nora whispered. "Give me thirty minutes. And call the state crime lab and coroner and tell them to get out there."

"You got it. Shit, this is terrible," Dave said.

"Terrible is what keeps us in business, Dave," Nora said. "I've got to get moving here."

As Nora hung up the phone, she wondered why she would make such a comment to Dave Henderson. She chalked it up to sleep-deprivation *ennui*. She poked at Randy.

"What? What?" he muttered.

"I've got to go to a crime scene," Nora said as she started getting dressed in the dark.

"Now, it's got to be..."

"One in the morning. I'm aware of that. If I'm not back by morning, get the kids off to school."

"Yeah. OK," Randy said as he burrowed back under the comforter.

She did not bother with her hair or makeup, but she made the time to brew herself some hot, black coffee. She needed it to lubricate her brain.

Cold blasted Nora as she stepped into the garage and started the car. For the money they had spent on this house, Nora thought, she wondered why they had avoided adding a heated garage. The car had a heavy feeling that it only has in winter. It creaks and moans like an old man, Nora thought as she backed out into the frozen darkness. Nora's red hair was matted, but she didn't care. She had covered her head with a thick wool hat and put on her red parka.

Route 14 was empty except for the drifting snow. This was a hell of a night to be fighting a fire and finding two dead bodies, Nora thought as she pulled into the Reynolds's farm.

The fire crew was cleaning up. Icicles hung from their helmets and suits. The Reynolds's farmhouse was almost completely burned down. It must have been burning a while before someone contacted the fire department, Nora observed. The air was filled with the smell of smoke and charred wood.

Dave Henderson—an eighteen-year veteran of the Lacroix

police force who liked to deal with things that he could handle easily— motioned to her to follow him into the smoldering wood pile. She could smell the bodies before she saw them, lying in the charred livingroom.

"Here they are. They're burned pretty bad, but it looks like each one was killed by a shotgun blast to the chest here in the livingroom. Then who ever did it set the fire to try to cover it up," he said.

"Do we know who called the fire in?" Nora asked.

"Dispatch said a person called it in shortly after eleven o'clock. Said he was driving by and saw the flames. He never identified himself. A good samaritan, I guess," Dave said.

"Maybe," Nora said. "Let's get pictures of the scene." She had brought her instant camera and began snapping photos of the bodies lying on the floor. The Reynolds's faces were turned to each other, as if they had wanted once last glance of the other before they lost consciousness. Nora noticed the remains of the family Christmas tree and its lights and ornaments in the corner. Some of the ornaments were floating in the puddles of water that had formed amidst the charred wooden beams of the house.

"Why were they killed here in the livingroom and not in their bedroom?" Nora said. "If it was a robbery gone bad, you would think that the thief would have waited until they had gone to bed. Most people who are startled by an intruder are asleep in their bedroom."

"That's a bit queer. You're right about that," Dave said.

"We need the crime scene boys to try to find some evidence of who might have been here," Nora said. "Although I don't know what they might find in this mess."

"Hell of a night, isn't it? And Christmas just a few days away," Dave said.

"Do we know if they have any children or relatives?" Nora said.

"Yeah, one of the fireman grew up out here. Says that they have five children and fifteen grandchildren. It was Judd Reynolds's family farm--over three hundred acres. He must have been seventy-five years old. Miriam was probably near the same age. One of his boys—Caleb—runs the farm now that Judd was getting up there in years. Hell of a thing. I suppose you're going to let Caleb and the rest of the family know what happened?"

"I guess I have to, Dave. That's why I joined the police force: to tell people that their loved ones had been brutally murdered," Nora said.

"I really don't know what you mean, Nora," Dave said. He had never seen Nora act this way.

"Forget it, Dave. I'm sorry. It's late. I'm freezing. You're freezing. Go sit in your car and warm up. I'll get Frank to drive out and give you a break so that you can go back to the station. Let's spread the misery," Nora said.

She walked back to her car. Her nose and ears had begun to freeze. You could almost hear the temperature dropping like a brick on a wooden floor.

CHAPTER 5

Bulldozers and other heavy earthmoving equipment sat idle in the farm fields west of Lacroix. They had ripped up and reshaped hundreds of acres where corn and soybeans once had grown. The land was now being prepared for a new crop, a human crop—rural settlers who sought a serene, bucolic existence far from the pressures of big cities.

The vision was nurtured by Lacroix's most famous son— the prolific artist Thomas Conrad. The son of a high school art teacher, Conrad left Lacroix twenty years ago, but he had recently returned. He built the most lavish house and studio on the largest lot in Lacroix. He also moved his art empire from suburban Chicago to Lacroix--the place, he declared in the local paper, "where all of my inspiration springs."

Before his momentous return, however, he had studied at the Art Institute of Chicago and then he began a career in advertising. His business career was short lived. Nearly simultaneously, he discovered God and the woman who would become his wife and muse. Lauren Van Moss convinced him to embrace God and to marry her. Thomas Conrad had found a woman to be the mother of his children and a calling that would make him famous.

For Conrad, the soul was the golden key to all human existence. The soul of serenity seeped through his paintings of farmhouses on a winter night and gently rolling hills on a crisp autumn day straight into the fibers of his loyal cadre of collectors around the world. Have a bad day at the office? Buy a Conrad, and then reflect and gain strength through serenity. Divorced? Pray for a better life at the foot of a Conrad painting that hangs in your den. Some collectors had over one hundred Conrads—as they lovingly called the paintings—

hanging in their homes. They would tell anyone who would listen that the works of Conrad changed their lives.

Thomas Conrad was the strip mall Picasso, and the online Monet. Both loyal collectors and new apostles could choose from a dizzying array of themes: bridges, churches, cottages, gazebos, hearths, lighthouse and gardens—all rendered with Conrad's signature nostalgic luminescence.

In spite of being scorned and lampooned by art critics in New York and Chicago, Conrad had become wealthy and famous. His bowling ball head with its neatly trimmed black beard and pear-like physique graced the covers of several national news magazines. His demeanor—equal parts serene and savvy—was transmitted to the American public on several television programs. His silent and adoring wife Lauren often looked on as he spoke of his vision for capturing the essence of the American experience.

It was now time to take the Conrad crusade to the next logical stage—from paintings to real places that people could touch and feel and live in. People could enter the places that once had hung on their walls. They could be enveloped by the soul of the soil. They could be part of the community of Placid, finding peace and fulfillment.

This was Thomas Conrad's ultimate artistic vision and carefully concocted business plan. To render real his vision, Conrad had solicited the help of his childhood friend—Lacroix real estate developer George Udelhoven. Placid would be Udelhoven's Notre Dame, his St. Peter's, his Chartres—standing forever and inspiring awe and reverence. It wouldn't be just a real estate development; it would be his legacy to the people of Lacroix and to the world.

At the end of each day, regardless of the weather, Udelhoven drove to the site of the Placid development west of town. In the numbing cold of December, some might say that the setting was uninviting and bleak. But to George, it was a glorious canvas--his canvas. His tools were different than those of his friend Tom, but his aim was just as high, just as noble. As the setting winter sun created long shadows that pierced the fields, George Udelhoven thought to himself that this place in his hands could become a masterpiece to rival anything that his old friend Tom had created.

CHAPTER 6

Looking at herself in the mirror of the second floor men's bathroom at Miller Publishing, Teresa Gonzalez began to cry. This is not what she had wanted for her life at the age of nineteen—to be cleaning men's shit and pubic hairs out of urinals and toilets in Lacroix. She wanted to be dancing at a steamy Latin nightclub in Chicago where she had been born. She wanted to dress sexy like the Latina stars she read about and watched on television. She wanted a dark, lanky man who smelled good to run his hands over her breasts and down between her legs.

But what man would be attracted to her now, she thought. Her hair was covered in a dark blue bandana and her body was encased in an old sweatshirt and ill-fitting jeans. She wiped a tear from her face with the fingers of her yellow rubber gloves.

"Teresa!" her mother Maria yelled. "Are you done in there yet? We are falling behind. We still need to vacuum and dust the entire second floor."

"I'm coming. I'm just about done," Teresa said, as she continued cleaning the bathroom stalls.

One year ago, Teresa's mother had brought her to Lacroix from Chicago to find work and live a better life, away from the street gangs and the desperation of the city's near South Side. She had read about Lacroix in an article in the *Chicago Tribune* about hidden travel treasures in the midwest. She was attracted by the rolling hills plummeting down to the river. It was such a contrast to the flatness and concrete of Chicago. She clipped the article and reread it almost every week. One day she decided to sell everything that couldn't be packed into her car and drive to Lacroix with Teresa in tow. Her neighbors in the Little Village neighborhood of Chicago didn't know what to make of her. Many had branded her "loco" after her husband Manny died in a car accident on the Dan Ryan Expressway when Teresa was only ten years old. But Maria was determined. She believed that this is what God wanted for her and Teresa. When she crossed the bridge over the Mississippi on a crisp autumn day a year ago in an old Buick, it was as if she had crossed into the promised land.

Maria and Teresa soon found work as cleaning ladies for Midwest Maids. Bud Baer, the owner and founder of Midwest Maids, advertised jobs that had reasonable hours and good pay. During the interview he had promised them that their working day would end at three in the afternoon. But after just a few days on the job, Maria and Teresa realized that, although their hourly wages ended at three o'clock, they were rarely finished cleaning up and putting away their supplies until after four o'clock, and sometimes not until five o'clock. Bud Baer had figured out how to get unpaid extra work from his employees.

After four months at Midwest Maids, Maria heard from her coworker Doris, who had heard it from a friend of hers who works at one of the law firms that Midwest Maids services, that Midwest Maids charged their clients twenty dollars an hour but paid their employees only six dollars. Besides the low pay, Maria didn't like Bud's rules for cleaning. He insisted that the floors should be cleaned with just a half bucket of lukewarm water. Maria realized that after a few minutes, she was just redistributing the dirty water over the floor. She couldn't stand this. Good cleaning required lots of hot water and soap, Maria believed.

So Maria decided that she and Teresa could do better on their own. They quit Midwest Maids. They were able to find a few residential and commercial customers through word of mouth. In a few weeks, by undercutting Midwest Maids' fees, they had enough regular customers to keep both of them busy.

Hispanic workers were still relatively uncommon in Lacroix. Whatever latent racism or suspicion the people of Lacroix harbored for someone with a non-European surname, these feelings were soon replaced with acceptance when Maria and Teresa proved that they were tireless workers who charged a reasonable price and who left a house or office spotless. Even though she had a bad back, Maria was from the old school: you cleaned floors on your hands and knees and you scrubbed hard.

Maria and Teresa saved enough money to move out of the motel near the highway and into a small two-bedroom apartment on Sixth Street in Lacroix's old downtown, near the river and the abandoned McGee boiler factory. Once a bustling neighborhood of German and Irish families who worked in nearby factories large and small, Sixth Street had declined into a series of deteriorating single-family homes that had been converted into apartments. Most of the tenants were divorced welfare mothers, unemployed car mechanics and students from St. Francis College who wanted to move out of their parents' house but still live cheaply.

Maria and Teresa furnished their apartment by shopping at garage sales and at the Salvation Army. When they needed extra food, they went to the food bank at St. Thomas Aquinas church.

"It's small, but it's better than we had in Chicago," Maria reminded Teresa whenever Teresa began to complain about the cramped surroundings. Except for a lack of cockroaches and mice, Teresa didn't see much of a difference in their home. Everything still seemed dreary. Her life on the job was hard and dirty, and her life at home was tedious and unexciting.

While Teresa dreamed of a different life, Maria worked like a whirlwind, not taking the time to formulate an opinion about her circumstances. Thinking too much was a luxury for wealthy people she would say. She would return home exhausted and lie down for hours on the small bed in her bedroom. Teresa decided that she needed to help her mother do the most difficult cleaning tasks that involved lifting vacuum cleaners up stairs or moving furniture.

When they were not working, they were resting or watching TV in their apartment. On Sundays at nine o'clock, Maria insisted that they attend Catholic mass at St. Raphael's Cathedral. One of the things that Maria liked best about Lacroix was the number of

Catholic churches. The sight of steeples and the sound of church bells on Sunday mornings lifted Maria's spirits. "God has brought us to this place," she would remind Teresa.

"God has not answered my prayers," Teresa thought as she walked out of the men's bathroom and joined her mother in the second floor hallway. She noticed that Maria was stretching her back and breathing heavily. "God, grant me the strength to change the way we live," Teresa murmured quietly.

"Mama, let me do the vacuuming. You rest for a while. You need to take a break," Teresa said.

"Maybe just a little one," Maria said, sitting down at the desk of an editor. Maria noticed that the editor had two small children—two girls. She carefully picked up the picture and smiled at the faces in the photograph. "People are so happy here. It's a better place," she thought.

CHAPTER 7

Teresa's life was the same every day. What she hated most, she decided, was not the dirt or the smells but the monotony. When she wasn't scrubbing the floor on her hands and knees in a position of primal submission, she was cleaning shit from toilets. There was shit on the seat and in the bowl and urine stains on the floors. "People are so disgusting," she told her mother, "when they know that someone else will clean up after them."

"Thank God you have the work to do," Maria would respond.

As she watched her mother clean someone's floor silently, Teresa wondered if her mother ever had dreams beyond this or if she really was as happy as she proclaimed. "Maybe I ask for too much out of life," Teresa sometimes thought.

But then she quickly determined that she was not asking for too much. For the occasional diversion, she would go upstairs to talk to and watch TV with Anastasia Schmidt, whom she had met in the laundry room a few weeks ago. Anastasia told Teresa to call her Anna.

A native of Lacroix, Anna had what school counselors would classify as a troubled home life. Her father regularly beat her with his belt when he was in a beer-and-Jack Daniels-induced rage. He saved his most severe punishment for her mother, whom he once hit in the head with a baseball bat. One night when she was fourteen, her mother shot her father in the head, then turned the gun on herself. For the rest of her high school years, Anna lived with her Aunt Sara. In her junior year in high school, Anna became pregnant by her volleyball coach, whom she had tried to seduce just for the sport of it. He quietly paid for her abortion and gave her five hundred dollars to keep quiet. In spite of this hush money, Anna sent an anonymous note to his wife, who turned her philandering husband in to the school principal and then divorced him. The coach quietly resigned from his post and moved away. Anna denied any knowledge of the note. Anna liked the power her blond hair and lean, muscular body could have over males, whether they were teenagers or married men. "I can eat men alive with my pussy," she often bragged.

Teresa was lucky to find Anna at home. Sometimes she would be gone for days. Teresa never bothered to probe too deeply into Anna's life. She didn't want her inquisitiveness to jeopardize a blossoming friendship—the only one she had in Lacroix. All Teresa knew was that Anna worked nights as a cocktail waitress at a bar called Howl across the river in Belleview.

"You know that they have some openings at Howl. You can make fifty or a hundred bucks a night in tips," Anna explained as she took a drag from her cigarette and curled up under a blanket on the sofa. Her apartment never seemed to have enough heat, and the temperature outside was near zero degrees.

"You're pretty. I'm sure that Hal—he's the owner—would snap you up in a minute. And you'd get to wear something other than a pair of fucking jeans and a sweatshirt," Anna said.

Teresa had never seen the outfit that Anna wore at work, although Anna explained that it was a little revealing. "More tits equal more money," she said. "And unless I'm mistaken, you got some tits there."

"I'm not sure about working in a place like that. I need to help my mother. She's getting old and can't do as much as she used to," Teresa said.

"Look at it this way," Anna said. "The more you make the less your mom has to clean shit. Give it some thought. Fifty bucks a night just serving drinks and wiggling your ass. It's easy money. And you'll meet some hot guys. When's the last time you were fucked?"

"Not since I've been here, that's for sure," Teresa said, as she glanced at the Enrique Iglesias video on the TV.

"Well, it's time you get back in the game. I can't go for more than a few weeks without the feel of a nice hard cock," Anna said. "I don't know how you can stand it."

"What time could I come by to meet your boss?" Teresa asked in a concerted attempt to change the subject from genitalia.

"How about this Saturday afternoon? Around six o'clock before things get crazy there. The dump opens at seven. I'll set everything up with Hal," Anna said.

Teresa began thinking of an excuse should would give her mother for borrowing the car.

"OK. I'll be there. Thanks."

"That's great. We'll have so much fun together. Man, that Enrique has one fine ass. You Latinos really know a thing or two about sex."

CHAPTER 8

The newsroom of the *Lacroix Herald* was crackling with an abnormal energy when Declan arrived in the morning. Everyone was talking about the Reynolds murder. Typical news fare for the paper involved stories on car accidents, house thefts or the occasional personal bankruptcy. A murder increased everyone's journalistic energy level. Even news crews and reporters from the state capital had arrived in Lacroix to cover the story.

"Phil, can't we get statements from any of the police except for Officer Dave Henderson? He didn't really tell you anything," Declan complained as he read a draft of Phil Haslett's front page story for the afternoon edition.

"He was the first officer at the scene," Phil said.

"But he says nothing that we don't already know," Declan said. "Who's the detective on the case?"

"It's Nora Morrissey. The only other detective on the force is Sam Langhoff, and he's on indefinite leave because of cancer treatments. So Nora it is. And she had nothing to say," Phil said.

"She always had something to say when I knew her," Declan said under his breath.

"What's that?" Phil asked.

"Nothing," Declan said. "Let me give Nora a call. We graduated from the same class at Lacroix High. She might open up more to an old high school pal. Why don't you work with Laura on the family tragedy angle of the story. You know, large loving family loses parents and grandparents close to the holidays, and so on."

"Got it," Phil said. "Make our readers weep."

Declan dialed the Lacroix police headquarters and asked for Nora. He was surprised that he got through so easily.

"Morrissey here," she said.

"Nora, Declan O'Brien here."

"Well, is it now. Is this official press business, or are you calling just to torture me?" she asked.

"Nice to talk to you again, too," Declan said.

"I saw that you had returned to our fair town. Was Chicago too big for you after all?"

"No, the city wasn't too big, but my marriage to Kate was too small. We got divorced last spring."

"Congratulations. I'm very happy for you."

"I think you're mixing up life events. Congratulations are for weddings, not divorces."

"I stand by my statement."

"Actually, to return to your first snide comment, I am calling on official press business," Declan said, not wanting to continue the personal direction in which the conversation was heading. "What can you tell me about where the investigation into the Reynolds murder stands? You wouldn't talk to my reporter Phil Haslett. I thought maybe you'd take mercy on me, for old times' sake. I'm coming up on a deadline."

"Phil's an idiot. I can't believe he's a journalist," Nora said.

"That's probably why he's working here in Lacroix. Anyway, can you tell me anything?"

"We have no suspects at the present time. All we know is that the Reynolds were shot at close range with a shotgun and that the murderer then set fire to their house to try to cover up the crime," Nora said flatly.

"You said 'murderer,'" Declan said. "Do you have evidence that there was just one murderer?"

"We're not sure that this point," Nora said. "Don't read anything into my use of the singular noun."

"Isn't trying to set fire to a house to cover up a crime pretty sophomoric, given today's forensic technology?" Declan said.

"I don't know what to think at this point. That's why we call it an investigation. I'm still investigating things. But I will say for the record that we will catch the killer or killers. Lacroix is not that big of a town. I doubt if the shooter came from very far away. They usually don't. Unless the Reynolds were part of some Colombian drug cartel, my guess is that the murderer lives right around here. Uh, please leave the stuff about the drug cartel out of your story. I was just making a point," Nora said.

"I understand your brand of sarcasm, Nora," Declan said. "I'll stick to the your official non-committal police-speak."

"You're so kind," Nora said. "Is there anything else? My job is solving crimes, not yacking on the phone, you know."

"Would you like to get together for lunch sometime since I'm back as an official resident of Lacroix? Wouldn't you like to interrogate me about a few things?" Declan said.

"I'm very busy," Nora said.

"Come on, just lunch. Even Sherlock Holmes took time out to dine," Declan said.

"OK. How about Thursday at eleven thirty at the Shot Tower," Nora said. "But only if nothing important comes up. Police business first. Slinging personal barbs second."

"Understood. The Shot Tower, eh? That place is still in business?" Declan said.

"You've got to get out more," Nora said. "Eleven-thirty on Thursday."

"I'll be there. I'll expect you to have captured the killer by then," Declan said.

"You always had too high expectations of me," Nora said.

Declan hung up the phone and called Phil over. "Here. I wrote down some quotes from Detective Morrissey for the story."

"Get anything good?" Phil asked, glancing at the scribbled notes.

"Not really, "Declan said.

"I guess high school friendships don't account for that much after all."

CHAPTER 9

Mayor Ellen Norberg sat in her livingroom sipping a lite beer and reading the evening *Lacroix Herald* that had just been launched onto her porch from the hand of the paperboy who lived two blocks away. Like everyone in Lacroix, she was devouring every detail about the brutal murder of Judd and Miriam Reynolds.

Unlike most people in Lacroix who read the news like it was a fiction thriller—titillating for a moment but then forgotten amidst the myriad other short-term enthusiasms of contemporary life—Ellen Norberg expressed deep concern to her husband Dr. Harry Norberg, who owned the town's most successful podiatry practice.

"Shit, Harry, murders aren't supposed to happen in Lacroix. Not now, when we've got Thomas Conrad's Placid development going," Ellen said. Just that afternoon, she had sat in on a marketing presentation for Placid that featured the slogan "Where Time Stands Still" printed over one of Conrad's rural paintings. "This could really kill us," Ellen added.

"An interesting choice of words," Harry said, looking up from the television.

"You know what I mean. We want people from Chicago and Minneapolis—people with means—to come and settle here and revitalize the city. We can't have this kind of bad publicity," Ellen said.

"They say that there's no such thing as bad publicity," Harry said.

"Shut up, Harry. Why do I even talk to you about this?" Ellen barked sarcastically.

"My feelings exactly," Harry said, getting out of his chair. "I'm heading out."

"Fine. Have a few beers on me," Ellen said.

"I always do," Harry said.

"Cut off anyone's toes today?" Ellen snorted.

Harry didn't respond. He knew that Ellen was baiting him. Two months ago Ellen personally paid off one of Harry's patients who had threatened to sue him, claiming that Harry had botched surgery to repair a club foot. A lawsuit would have been personally embarrassing and politically damaging to Ellen. Harry wanted to contest the lawsuit. He believed that he had done nothing wrong. Then Ellen took over and resolved the situation before any odor of scandal could drift into the constantly sniffing noses of reporters or political enemies.

After Harry had left, Ellen called Alan Harrison, who taught music at St. Francis College and conducted the Lacroix Chamber Orchestra.

"Harry's left for the evening. Can I come over? I'm upset about these murders," she said.

"I'll be here," Harrison said.

"Have your violin ready. I want the Bach."

"Of course you do. I'm getting it in tune now."

"Give me fifteen minutes."

CHAPTER 10

Ellen looked at her naked body in Alan Harrison's full-length antique mirror. She decided that she didn't look bad for a forty-five-year-old woman who had given birth to two children. She still retained much of her athletic physique from her high school and college days as a softball player. Her long legs still were muscular. She slid her hand over her hips, which were only slightly wider than they had been during her playing days. Her upper frame was solid without being too masculine. Her ample breasts thrust majestically outward. She smoothed back her shoulder-length blond hair.

When she began her political career ten years ago with her election to the Lacroix city council, she decided to change her hair from dark brown to blond. She felt that it made her look younger and more attractive—two key components for an ambitious female politician, she had decided. Her change in hair color also ignited a new era in erotic adventures. Harry was becoming less of a reliable and interesting lover. So Ellen sought out other intriguing, powerful and, most important, discreet men who could satisfy her desires while not compromising her place in the public political arena. She had long abandoned any desire for sensual tenderness. She now craved just raw animal sexuality.

She had met Professor Alan Harrison six months ago at the dedication of a new concert hall at St. Francis College—her alma mater. Alan was a soloist in one of Mozart's violin concertos. Ellen couldn't take her eyes off a man whose body swayed gently as he played Mozart's intoxicating melodies. She noticed his delicate fingers caressing the strings and wondered what his fingers would feel like stroking her skin, playing her like an instrument.

When she learned that he was twice divorced and living alone in a vintage Victorian house near the campus, she decided to invite him to dinner to discuss a possible donation to the music department. That night, she learned what a great musician he really was.

Ellen glided her bare feet across the hardwood floor of Alan's bedroom and kneeled on a pillow that he had placed near the fireplace. Except for the light from the fire, the room was completely dark. Ellen could feel the heat from the fire on her backside. Alan stood before her naked and began to play Bach's violin sonata in G minor. Ellen took his penis into her mouth as he played. She put her right hand between her legs and stroked herself softly as the music filled the darkened room.

As his erection grew, she knew that he would not be able to concentrate on Bach much longer. She pushed him to the floor. She then mounted him with a quick, confident movement. His fingers moved up and down her back, stroking with increased urgency as she began to moan louder. He thrust his hips violently upwards. Ellen cupped her hands around his neck and mirrored his pelvic movements until the bonfire in her spine made her nearly faint. She rolled off of him and grabbed a blanket to cover them. They stared at the ceiling and caught their breath. Neither one spoke for several minutes.

"I need a drink," she said, breaking the silence.

"Are there any leads on the murders?" Alan asked as he walked to the kitchen to pour a glass of wine.

"Not yet," Ellen replied, raising her voice so that Alan could hear her.

"When's the last time there was a murder here?" Alan said, returning with a glass of expensive French red wine that he ordered special on an internet web site.

"Ten years ago. One of our local town drunks was found beaten by the freight tracks. It was never solved. And no one cared that he had been killed anyway. But this is different, and more serious."

"Should I be worried?"

"About your shares in the Placid development?"

"Yes."

"No. Your investment will pay off. The Placid development won't be derailed by this. I'll make sure of it. I have too much to lose myself."

"Don't you mean the community has too much to lose?"

"You heard what I said. Hugh O'Neill is retiring from the state senate next year, and I plan on winning his seat. The Placid deal is my ticket out of Lacroix and to the state capital. And let me remind you that the state university pays more than St. Francis College. I'm sure that I could have a conversation with the music school dean about your unique qualifications."

"That sounds interesting. And I thought patronage died with the Baroque era," Alan said as he began kissing her breasts.

Ellen's cell phone began ringing.

"Fuck," she said.

"Let it ring."

"No, it could be some news about the murder investigation," she said. Ellen stood up and found her phone amidst her tangled clothes.

"I have to go," she said. "There's been another murder. A woman named Bennington."

"Let the police handle it. I'll play Vivaldi for you if you stay."

"That sounds nice. But I have to go. I handle everything in Lacroix," Ellen said. "I'll call you when I have time. Maybe we can get together after the Christmas concert."

"I'll keep practicing."

CHAPTER 11

Nora looked at the picture of a beautiful woman with glowing red hair and hazel eyes holding her daughter, who had inherited her mother's vibrant hair color. She couldn't reconcile such a peaceful image with the bloody mess on the oriental rug in the living room of a gorgeous brick house surrounded by towering oak trees.

"How's the little girl?" Nora asked Stan Richards, the police officer who had been the first person on the scene.

"The neighbor, a Leigh Fortunata, is taking care of Paris—that's her name—until we can get family services over here in the morning," Officer Richards said.

"Was she hurt in any way?" Nora said.

"Not that we can tell. But I'll be escorting Mrs. Fortunata to the hospital so that the girl can be checked out. It looks like she had been here all alone with her dead mother since she got up this morning. At least that's what it looks like. Sad story," Richards said.

"Who called this in?' Nora said.

"Mrs. Fortunata. Ms. Bennington was supposed to take Paris over to the Fortunata house earlier this afternoon to play with Mrs. Fortunata's daughter. When Ms. Bennington didn't show up or answer the phone, Mrs. Fortunata went over to knock on the door. No one answered, but she thought she could here the little girl crying. That's when she became concerned and called 911," Richards explained.

"OK. So what do we have here?" Nora said, forcing herself to look more closely at Christa Bennington's battered face.

"It looks like she was beaten severely with something like a hammer. Whoever did this was pretty angry. Her skull is smashed in something awful," Richards said.

"That's for sure. Pretty sick," Nora said. "Any sign of forced entry?"

"No, the front door was shut and locked. All of the other doors and windows were OK."

"So either the killer had a key or knew where Bennington kept hers. How about fingerprints or footprints?"

"The sidewalk had recently been shoveled, so no footprints in the snow. And I didn't notice anything on the wood floor or rug. But the state crime lab people are on their way. Good thing that they were still here for the Reynolds case."

"Yeah, good thing," Nora said.

"I've lived here all of my life and no one, except that bum by the tracks, had ever been murdered. Now three people in two days," Richards said. "This only happens in big cities like Chicago."

"I guess Lacroix is coming up in the world," Nora said. "Did Bennington have any family besides her daughter?"

"According to Mrs. Fortunata, both her parents are dead. The mother just passed on a few months ago—cancer I think. But she has a sister Allison who lives in San Francisco."

"I'll call the sister. How about an ex-husband, anything like that?"

"Not according to Mrs. Fortunata."

"Well, some guy is the father of her child."

"Mrs. Fortunata said that Bennington didn't talk about who the father was. Maybe it was a married lover or one of those sperm donor things like the rich celebrities do."

"Maybe. Maybe not, Stan. All the more reason to find who he is and where he is, if he exists at all. Maybe there's some kind of ugly custody fight going on. Anyway, I think I need to speak with Mrs. Fortunata myself," Nora said. "Keep everyone out of here until the crime lab is through."

"Will do. This is a really nice house. It's a pity that something so brutal would happen here," Richards said. "What do you think this place is worth?"

"I don't know Stan. Why don't you call an appraiser while you're waiting. Or maybe you can find Christa Bennington's mortgage files around here someplace," Nora said. "Don't forget that we have a murder victim on the floor over there."

"I didn't mean any disrespect. I was just…"

"Shut up, Stan," Nora said as she left the house and to have a conversation with Mrs. Fortunata.

CHAPTER 12

Leigh Fortunata sat on the sofa as Nora talked to her about Christa Bennington. Her husband Sam owned four liquor stores in Lacroix and had done very well for someone who had dropped out of college during his sophomore year.

"Thank you for taking in the little girl. Officer Richards will be over here in a few minutes to take you and the girl to the hospital so that a doctor can check her out," Nora said.

"She looks OK. She's just scared. And asking for her mommy. She's upstairs with my two daughters and my husband Sam," Leigh explained as she began to cry. "I just can't believe what happened. And right next door. I should have seen something, or heard something. Oh, my God, has anyone contacted Christa's sister Allison? I think she lives in San Francisco."

"Yes, I've left her a message, but I haven't heard back from her yet. But don't blame yourself, Mrs. Fortunata. How long had you known Christa?" Nora asked.

"Since she moved in with her mother about four years ago. Rose Bennington was a dear lady. She just died in September. She had some kind of cancer—lung cancer I think. Christa left her job in New York City to come home. I think she was writing a book or something. She was so pretty, so glamorous," Leigh said. "She would bring Rose out to the backyard, and Rose would sit in a chair watching Christa play with Paris. Rose was so proud of her grandchild."

"Now, Mrs. Fortunata, help me understand something. Who is Paris's father?" Nora asked.

"Christa would never tell me. I asked on several occasions, but she just said it was some man whom she no longer wanted to see. Maybe she told her sister something."

"I'll be asking her sister the same question. But let's get back to this man. Was he from Lacroix? This town isn't that big, and someone as attractive and sophisticated as Christa Bennington would certainly be remembered at bars or restaurants," Nora said.

"I don't know, Detective Morrissey. I wish I did know. Maybe he wasn't from around here. I just don't know and I stopped asking. Figured it wasn't my business," Leigh said.

"How about harassing phone calls, or men who might have been bothering her?"

"She never mentioned anything like that to me."

"OK. OK. Now you were at home last night?"

"Yes. Both Sam and I were, along with our girls."

"You didn't see or hear anything out of the ordinary?"

"No. It's been so cold that we just stay in, light a fire and watch TV."

"So you didn't hear any weird noises or maybe a car speeding away? Or you didn't see anyone sitting in a parked car?"

"No. Sorry. I didn't hear anything. It was just like any other night. But when Christa didn't bring Paris over to play with my Rachel this afternoon, I went over. That's when I heard Paris crying and called the police."

"You didn't see anything on the porch. Something that might have been dropped?"

"No. Nothing. I wish I could be more helpful."

The doorbell rang.

"That's probably Officer Richards. Thank you very much for your time. And I'm very sorry about Ms. Bennington," Nora said. "Please call me if you or Sam remember anything."

"We will. Please catch the guy who killed Christa," Leigh said as she opened the door for Officer Richards.

As she left Leigh Fortunata and walked back to the Bennington house where the crime lab team had just arrived, Nora thought about Leigh's departing comment about "catching the guy." "I guess it's only natural to think that a man was the killer. Murderers are typically men," Nora said to herself. But her father had trained her never to settle for the obvious. She quickly walked up the steps as a brisk wind picked up, throwing fine shards of frozen snow into her face.

CHAPTER 13

Teresa pulled into the parking lot of Howl just before six o'clock in the evening. There were three other cars parked in the gravel lot. Frozen piles of dirty snow had been stacked to one side of the lot, which was dimly lit except for the red neon sign that was shaped like a pouncing wolf on the front of bar. The long, narrow building was made of logs and looked to Teresa like some kind of hunting lodge.

Anna had told her to go around to the employee entrance in the back and ask for the owner Hal. Teresa wore her newest pair of jeans, leather boots and a white sweater that accentuated her breasts. She was nervous, but she was also determined to exhibit a sense of calm to whomever she spoke.

She walked into a backroom, but on one was there. All she could hear was the sound of clanking glasses and plates coming from an invisible kitchen. She then walked out into the main bar, which had a runway down the center and small tables placed around it. Along the wood-paneled walls were semicircular booths. She noticed a man talking on a cell phone behind the long wooden bar. He waved to her to come over.

As Teresa got closer to him, she saw that he was wearing a red T-shirt that had the words "Primal Scream" placed underneath the wolf logo of Howl. His face was lopsided, like a misshapen pumpkin. His greying black hair was pulled into a tight ponytail.

"Yes, sir. I can get you and your party into the VIP room at ten o'clock. No problem. Anna and Lily will be available. No problem. I look forward to seeing you again," the man said as he hung up the phone.

"And what can I do you for, honey?" the man asked as he scanned Teresa up and down.

"I'm looking for Hal. My friend Anna said that she had set up an interview with him. I'm Teresa Gonzalez."

"Welcome to Howl, Teresa. I'm Hal. So this is the place. Have you ever worked at a gentleman's club before?"

"No," Teresa admitted. "But I'm sure than I could learn from Anna."

"You can learn a lot of things from Anna. What are you doing now?"

"I work with my mother cleaning homes and offices in Lacroix. I would like to make some extra money to help my mother," Teresa said.

"That's as good a reason as any that I've heard recently. Well, you're an attractive girl and Anna had good things to say about you. I think my clients would really go for you. So do you want to hostess or perform?"

"I'm sorry. I don't understand."

"This is a strip club, honey. Girls take their clothes off here. Anna takes her clothes off here. You can't tell me that you hadn't figured that out?" Hal said, laughing.

Teresa was too embarrassed to answer immediately. She felt naïve and stupid, but she told herself to remain poised. Of course, this was a strip club. If she had only read between the lines of what Anna had been describing. Anna was always telling her that she had a great body and that sex meant power and opportunity if used wisely and shrewdly. Teresa couldn't take another day of scrubbing floor and toilets so she didn't care that Howl was a strip club.

"I wasn't sure. But that's OK with me," Teresa said, maintaining her composure. "I'd like to start as a hostess, I guess."

"That's great, honey. You'll get minimum wage plus tips," Hal said. "The hours are seven at night until three in the morning. Can you start next week? On Monday night?"

"Yes, I think I can."

"Anna or one of the other girls will get you fixed up with one of our outfits. The cost of the uniform will come out of your first check," Hal explained.

"OK."

"So do you have any questions?"

"No. Just thank you for the job."

"The pleasure's all mine, " Hal said. "So I'll see you Saturday night. This place will be rockin' then."

As Teresa drove out of the lot and back across the bridge to Lacroix, she began to form a variety of explanations for her mother. Nothing seemed to sound right. She decided that she needed to talk to Anna again—about a lot of things.

CHAPTER 14

Declan sat at a corner table of the Shot Tower, waiting for Nora to arrive. A few lunchtime patrons who worked at nearby businesses were coming in. The restaurant began to reverberate with the sounds of booming, garrulous midwestern voices and laughter. As he waited, Declan thought about all of the dozens, maybe hundreds of people, who float into and out of one's life and who leave no mark. And then there are those who seem to be with you night and day even though many years have passed between meetings. Nora was one of those people who linger, who remain stamped on you like a birthmark.

Declan could still smell the scent of her hair and the fresh aroma of her laundered clothes. He could hear her devilish laugh and her hearty screams. He could see the mole on her left thigh and the small scar on her right breast that she received after being bitten by a stray dog while at the beach when she was twelve years old. He could still feel her legs wrapped around his thighs and her soft breath in his ear.

Declan can also remember that he left Nora to go to college in Chicago while she went to the state college. He still replays the phone call on a January night from his dormitory when he said it was best that they went their separate ways because he wanted to explore the world and she was destined to remain in Lacroix. He didn't go to her wedding, and she didn't come to his. But yet she lingered.

"A quarter for your thoughts," Nora said as she sat down at Declan's table. "I figure that you're used to big city prices. That's why I didn't offer a penny."

"But I'm back in Lacroix now, so maybe a dime might be a good compromise," Declan said. "Thanks for keeping our appointment. I know things must be crazy with the Reynolds murder, and now there's the Christa Bennington case. Anything you can tell me about either investigation, on or off the record?"

"Yes, I'm sorry about your parents," she said, avouding his question. "I'm glad that I didn't have to handle the call. It was a terrible car accident. Your parents still had a lot of life left in them. I'm truly sorry, Declan—for you and Moira. How is your sister?"

"She's fine, thanks. She's prone to weeping jags every now and then, but otherwise she's doing fine. I appreciate your thoughts. You didn't come to the funeral," Declan said.

"I just couldn't do it. You must think I'm cold."

"No. Of course not. Death affects people differently. People can pay their respects to the dead alone in the quiet of their own thoughts without sharing it in public. Don't worry about it, Nora," Declan said.

"So now you're living alone in that big house," Nora said.

"Not entirely alone. I have a cat—Melville."

"Good Lord. Melville! Only you, Declan," Nora said, laughing.

"He's everything that my ex-wife wasn't—affectionate and quiet, " Declan said.

"Oh, yes, the ex-wife. What was her name again?"

"Kate."

"Yes, Kate. Like in *The Taming of the Shrew*. I was surprised that you got married in the first place."

"It was one destination I had yet to explore."

"Would you go back?"

"Too early to decide. The skid marks haven't healed yet. But can we talk about Christa Bennington for a few minutes?"

"There's not much I can tell you, or should tell you. She was murdered with a blunt instrument, leaving a sister and a daughter named Paris," Nora said.

"I've got reporters trying to find out who the father of her child is," Declan said.

"And I'm trying to do the same thing."

"Covering the murders of three people is not something I was expecting to do when I came back here," Declan said. "I wanted a place of peace and quiet where I could retire in monastic bliss."

"The day that you enter a monastery is the day I will rob a bank, Declan."

"So noted for the record. But I'm right that murders here in Lacroix are rare."

"Yes. These are the first murders that I've ever investigated. It's something I was trained to do, but not something I ever really wanted to do," Nora said.

"But you are Detective Morrissey, after all," Declan said. "You always wanted to be on the police force. And you did it, Nora. I admire that."

"You never told me that before."

"My mistake. How is Mr. Morrissey?"

"The car business is doing well. He can't wait for spring so he can play softball again. His team was the regional champion last year."

"Sounds like he lives a rich life."

"Don't be such a snob. Look around. You're at the Shot Tower in Lacroix about to order lunch." Nora said.

"Point taken. Sorry."

"I assume that you've been to France," Nora said, changing the subject.

"Yes, several times."

"Alone or with Kate."

"Both."

Nora paused and then said: "Let's eat. Tell me all about Paris and the French countryside. I especially want to hear about the warm French countryside on this cold winter day," Nora said.

"Sure, Nora. I'd be glad to. France has always been one of my favorite places."

As Declan told Nora about walking along a country road in

Arles just like Van Gogh once did, he could smell Nora's hair from across the table. He wanted to touch it. But he kept on telling his stories, because that was what Nora had asked him to do.

CHAPTER 15

The story made the front page of the *Lacroix Herald* and had appeared in many newspapers across the state and the midwest. Twenty years later, people in Lacroix would still talk about it as they swapped stories in bars or as they sat in the pews at St. Thomas Aquinas church, listening to their young pastor sermonize during Sunday mass. Father Joseph Knipfel had been struck by lightning on a golf course while playing in a tournament for the Lacroix High School golf team, and he had survived. His clothes and hair had been burned, but his heart kept on beating.

Even though he had been an altar boy at St. Thomas Aquinas before being struck by lightning, he had never considered himself as being particularly religious. To the contrary, his adolescence was routinely secular—the usual teenage drinking, brooding, sports playing and dating. Girls liked his breezy conversations, soft brown hair and gracefully elongated arms, hands and neck that earned him the moniker "The Swan."

At first, he thought the nickname was effeminate, and he bristled when anyone called him "The Swan" to his face. But after a while, he embraced the regal and sensual associations that the bird evoked. And he was absolutely sold on the water fowl after he had read William Butler Yeats's poem "Leda and the Swan" in English class. The poem recounts the Greek myth of Leda being ravished by Zeus in the form of a swan, but at a deeper level the poem suggests the struggle between free will and fate, the eruption of artistic vision and the depth of man's knowledge. To Joseph, the poem touched on subjects that also interested him: the lusty and the lofty. From then on, he saw the swan as being an appropriate symbol of the sensuous and the spiritual. He was glad when people called him by that name.

After the lightning strike, however, his direction in life took a dogleg right toward the lofty and the spiritual. That day changed him, he told his parents, teachers, coaches and friends. He decided to devote his life to God and the priesthood, although he still got in a round of golf or two with a few of his parishioners.

One of the few people who still playfully called him "The Swan," or these days "Father Swan," was his old high school friend Declan O'Brien, who sat across from him in his office in the church's rectory.

"I learned from Christa's neighbor Mrs. Fortunata that she went to church here," Declan said. "Is that true, Joe? Was she a regular church goer? I just want to get a sense of the person she was for the profile we're doing on her."

"Are you writing the story yourself, Declan? I thought you would have reporters to do this sort of thing, now that you're a big time city editor," Father Joseph said, laughing.

"That's right, I've hit the big time here in Lacroix. But with all that's been happening, I decided to dust off my notepad and handle this angle of the story myself. You know, mix it up on the mean streets of Lacroix," Declan said. "Seriously, though, it's not as if we have an army of reporters at the *Herald*, and we have two murder cases to investigate. Plus, I figured that you would be more comfortable talking to an old golfing buddy."

"I see. Yes, indeed. Well, Christa was one of my parishioners, for about the past four years. She didn't get too involved in parish activities, however. She was a quiet person, a guarded person who said she was trying to reconnect with the spiritual. That was more important to her I think than the parish community at large. I believe God gave her comfort during her mother's long illness."

"Did you know Rose Bennington well?"

"Not well, but I would make it a point to visit her once a week during the last few months when her cancer had progressed and she was near death. God rest her soul."

FIRE AND ICE

"Would you say that you knew Christa Bennington well?"

"As I said, Declan, she was a very private person. She asked me sometimes for reading suggestions. She liked Thomas Merton, for example. We had occasional talks about spirituality. But I wouldn't say that I knew her well. She liked her quiet, anonymous life here in Lacroix. I understand it was a sharp contrast from her prior career in New York City."

"That's an understatement, Joe. She was quite the social butterfly in the Big Apple," Declan said. "What about her daughter Paris? Did she ever talk about her father?"

"Not to me, no. All I knew is that she wasn't married and that the father wasn't around. But it certainly didn't adversely affect Paris. She's a delightful little girl," Father Joseph said.

"Weren't you curious, you know, in a nosy secular sort of way?" Declan said.

"Of course, you've got me there. But I didn't ask and she didn't tell."

"Or confess?"

"Nice try, Declan. But you know I can't answer that."

"But you can't fault me for trying. One more thing: Mrs. Fortunata said that you would sometimes help Christa with home repairs. What was that all about?"

"You know I like to build things, Declan. I help the workmen out here in the church if I can, not only to save money but because I just like carpentry. I'm the only priest I know who owns a toolbelt and has a rectory full of power tools. Sometimes I offered to help Christa out. Repair a railing here, fix an electrical outlet there. Things like that. Her house is very old. You know Jesus's father Joseph was a carpenter, Declan. You can't have forgotten all of your Bible studies."

"In spite of myself, I do remember something about carpentry in the New Testament, "Declan said. "But don't even think about trying to get my ass back into one of your finely sanded pews. I see that look in your eye."

"I wouldn't think of it," Father Joseph said.

"One last question, Joe. Do you have any idea who might have killed Christa Bennington?"

"Not a clue. I'm as shocked as anyone. Her murder is just senseless."

"Senseless enough to make you curse your God?"

"Nice try, Declan. But no. I believe in my God's goodness. But I do despair about man's capacity to hurt another human being."

"Don't we all," Declan said. "Thanks, Joe. I mean Father Swan, I mean Father Joseph, for your time. So what's next on your agenda today—a baptism, some plastering?"

"I'm glad that your sarcasm is still in tact, Declan. It's one of your annoyingly endearing qualities," Father Joseph said, rising from his chair and extending his hand to Declan.

"That's what my ex-wife thought as well. But I think she focused more on the annoying rather than on the endearing. Wives can be like that," Declan said.

"Why don't we talk more about things like that over a beer sometime," Father Joseph said.

"Will you take that white collar off?"

"If you're buying the drinks, I'll leave it here."

"You've got yourself a deal. I'll give you a call," Declan said. As he walked back to his car, he stopped and looked back at the red brick rectory nestled against the stately old church. He still couldn't reconcile the obvious fact that the golf team buddy with whom he used to go on dates, tell dirty jokes and watch hours of sports on TV was now a Catholic priest. He felt glad that the lightning had missed him.

CHAPTER 16

George Udelhoven noticed that in person Thomas Conrad's face was puffier than it was in the publicity photos for the Placid development. Tom had aged better than he had, George thought. Tom's shimmering blue eyes and perfectly combed brown hair—now peppered with just a hint of grey—evoked serenity and artistic vision. Tom was, George decided, the perfect salesman to lure a new breed of pioneers to a self-contained community where people could feel safe, far removed from a brutal and chaotic world.

"George, tell it to me straight, what do these murders in Lacroix do to our marketing efforts?" Tom said as he sat behind his desk in the office of his art warehouse in Lacroix's new business park.

"I'd be more concerned if our target audience lived in Lacroix or nearby. But I've checked the newspapers in Chicago, Minneapolis and a few other major cities, and nothing about the murders of the Reynolds or the Bennington woman has appeared. You know it as well as I do, Tom: those cities have their own crimes to worry about. Gangs and drugs and crap like that. They're not going to focus on a few killings here in little Lacroix. So don't worry, " George said reassuringly.

"But isn't the Reynolds's land adjacent to our site?" Tom said. "That's troubling. How are we going to purchase it now that they're dead. The acreage that they owned was key to the fulfillment of our vision."

"Yes, we had been talking to Judd Reynolds about selling his farm so that we could reach our acreage goal for Placid. We hadn't reached an agreement before he was killed. He was a tough old bird, and shrewd. He wouldn't settle for what we offered. And he didn't like the whole idea of the Placid community. But I think we'll have more luck with son Caleb, who's handling the estate," George explained. "I have some sources who tell me that Caleb's not much of a farmer and he likes to go to the riverboat casino and the greyhound park."

"Caleb's going to inherit the land?" Thomas said. "Are you sure?"

"He's the oldest son, so it would figure," George said. "But I'm not just guessing, Tom. I have some sources who have confirmed this."

"What kind of sources?"

"It's better that only I know these things, Tom. Your job is to be the upfront man, get on TV, spread your vision. I'll take care of the behind-the-scenes details," George said.

"So you'll think we'll be all right? Lauren and I have been dreaming about Placid for a long time. God has finally blessed us with the opportunity to see our vision come to life."

"You've got nothing to worry about," George said. "I've told you. We'll get this last piece of land secured. We're already started construction on the first parcels, and we have almost ninety percent of the lots sold. A little over a year from now, the first families will be moving into Placid. It will be everything you've imagined. And you'll make some good money as well. We both will. All of our investors will. This place is a gold mine."

"I don't like to talk about the village in those terms," Thomas said. "It sort of cheapens it, don't you think?"

Bullshit, George thought. You lying bastard with your net worth at over one hundred million dollars from selling truckloads of art like they were washers and dryers.

"Of course not. For you it's more than the investment. I understand that. But for me and the other working stiffs who put up some money, well we'd like to see a modest return," George said. "Look at the time. I've got a meeting with Mayor Norberg in an hour."

"Give Ellen my best. She's done a great job for Lacroix. This place has changed for the better in recent years. It has a new vitality without having lost its provincial charm," Thomas said. "It's really our home, isn't it, George?"

"You bet. Best damn town in the country. I'll let her know that you sent her your regards," George said.

Driving to city hall, he began to sweat even though the temperature was only a few degrees above zero. He turned down the heat in his Lexus and unzipped his heavy coat. He knew exactly what Ellen Norberg was going to say to him. He just had a few minutes to come up with a good answer.

CHAPTER 17

The two conversations Teresa had yesterday still played in her head as she drove to Howl for her first night of work. After learning about what really went on at Howl, she talked to Anna and asked her why she had not informed her that Howl was a strip club. Anna just laughed and wondered how a girl from Chicago could be so naïve. "So I strip. Big deal. I make good money and I enjoy it, " Anna had said. "You'll change your tune once you start making some real cash. Or do you want to go back and clean pee stains off tile floors? Should I tell Hal that you don't want the job?"

Teresa told Anna that she was going to take the job, but she had made her point that Anna should have been more honest. Anna hugged her and then offered her a beer.

Teresa's other conversation was with her mother, who sat in stunned silence when Teresa told her that she got a job being a waitress. Teresa didn't fill in the other details about what Howl served besides beer and mixed drinks. Teresa reassured her mother that she would continue cleaning with her as much that she could, but that this job would be a great opportunity to make more money, which could be used to find a better apartment and buy nicer things. Maria began to mumble prayers in Spanish and implored Teresa to be careful. Looking back on the conversation, Teresa was surprised that her mother had put up such a weak resistance.

Theresa drove across the bridge to Belleview. Houses and businesses displayed their holiday lights and decorations. One of the few buildings that did not have multi-colored lights or wreaths hanging from roofs or shrubbery was Howl. The building looked lost and sad, she thought. When Teresa arrived, the parking lot was half full—mostly with pickup trucks and SUVs. As she walked from her car to the employee entrance, she could hear the low pounding of the bass from the sound system coming through the walls. She thought she could see the building's walls move in and out, as if they were breathing. But she knew she must have been imagining things because she was so nervous. She wanted to turn around and return home. But return to what? Anna was right. This was the starting line to something better for her and her mother.

When she entered, she asked for Hal. A large man with a shaved head and a dragon tattoo on his neck asked who she was.

"Oh yeah, Teresa. I'm Vince. Hal told me to keep an eye out for you. You got your own locker through that door there. Hal's got your uniform and everything in there. He told me to remind you that the cost of the clothes is going to come out of your first check," the man said. "Some of the girls forget that."

"No, I remember what he said. But is someone going to show me what to do? How things work?" Teresa said.

"Does this place look like a nuclear power plant to you? You serve drinks. Hal or the other ladies will show you what to do. Just change and get going," Vince said.

"OK. Thanks," Teresa said meekly, not wanting to continue talking to Vince. She found her locker, on which her name was scribbled on a piece of masking tape. It was incorrectly spelled "Teresa." The dressing room looked like the girls' locker room from her high school back in Chicago: grey and decaying.

Anna had told her to bring a pair of black heels and that Hal would provide pants and a top. Anna wrote down Teresa's clothes size and told her that she would make sure that everything would fit.

What Anna found in her locker was a pair of tight-fitting black shorts and a low-cut white T-shirt with the word "Howl" and an outline of a wolf sown into the upper left. Teresa looked at herself in the mirror. The clothes couldn't have been any smaller, she thought. She adjusted her hair and lipstick and went out into the bar.

Howl's main room was nearly full. The music was deafening.

FIRE AND ICE

Two naked women were dancing on the runway, rubbing each other's breasts with something sticky—it looked to Teresa like honey—and then bending down so that the men in the front row could lick them.

Teresa saw Hal behind the bar.

"Teresa, honey. You look great. Really sexy. It's a busy night. Take those tables over there in the corner," Hal said.

"I'm a bit nervous. Is someone going to help me learn things?" Teresa asked.

"There's not much to learn. Go talk to Helene. She'll show you the ropes. Honey, I can't talk right now. The bar's crazy. You'll do fine. You look great. Really hot."

Teresa found Helene, who gave her the basics about the food and drink menu and how to use the cash register. "Just don't let these bastards paw at you," Helene said. "Our job is to serve drinks. If someone's hands start roving, you just tell Duke over there. He'll kick their ass."

The evening was a blur to Teresa. She was going back and forth between tables and the bar non-stop for hours. The noise of the music and the loud conversation made her head pound. Every fifteen or twenty minutes, another woman or pair of women would come on stage and perform. She kept looking for Anna, but she couldn't find her.

"Anna is working the VIP room tonight. Only Hal's favorites get to work there. The clientele is more refined than the drooling car mechanics and farm boys who come in here. Real professionals sit there. You know, doctors and lawyers. Men who should be at home with their wives. But Anna's been here a while. I guess she's earned it, " Helene explained.

The hours flew by--past one o'clock in the morning, and then two o'clock. Teresa's tips began to grow as the evening progressed. She was too busy to count the money until Howl finally closed at three o'clock in the morning. Back in the locker room, Teresa and the other women dressed in their regular clothes and counted their tip money. Teresa had earned over one hundred and fifty dollars in tips. She was stunned.

"You did great for your first night. I heard some men saying that they liked your dark Spanish looks. Actually, I heard them say that they wanted to fuck the Spanish chick. I won't bore you with the anatomical details of their insightful comments. But you definitely got something different going on than me and the other fake blondes here. You're exotic. Don't have much of that here in Lacroix," Helene said, smiling. She then took a long gulp of beer.

"Do you think Anna is still here? I want to tell her about my first night," Teresa said.

Helene and a few of the other women laughed.

"Anna left a while ago," Helene said. "She's long gone by now. She's someplace warm and comfy."

Teresa didn't know how to respond.

"Think about it while you drive home," Helene said as she gently stroked Teresa's hair.

CHAPTER 18

George Udelhoven could feel drips of perspiration form under his arms and on the top of his forehead as he pulled into the city hall parking lot. Ellen Norberg could do that to a man, he thought, even on a bitterly cold day like this.

Ellen's executive assistant Marianne asked him to wait for a few minutes. George had known Ellen since she first ran for city council ten years ago. Ellen had become more beautiful and more ruthless in those ten years, George thought. He wished that he wife Eileen had kept in shape like Ellen. As he sat in the waiting room, George indulged himself in a recurring fantasy of taking Ellen from behind in a large bed overlooking the Caribbean. He could hear her moans and feel the tight flesh of her butt in his hands.

"Mr. Udelhoven, Mayer Norberg can see you now," Marianne said.

"What? I'm sorry," George responded.

"Mayor Norberg. She's finished with her call. She can see you now."

"Sorry. I mean thanks."

Ellen was standing behind her desk dressed in a shapely black dress that accented her breasts and her athletic legs. George thought that her ensemble was more appropriate for after-dinner cocktails in the summer rather than for a town's chief executive in December with Christmas only a few days away.

"Have a seat, George," Ellen said.

Glancing at the well-appointed Christmas tree in the corner of her office, George commented: "That's a lovely tree. Did Marianne decorate it for you?'

"Fuck the holiday cheer, George. Are we at risk because of the murder of that farm couple—the Reynolds? I don't plan on losing my investment in the Placid Partnership. And more than the money, the development is going to be my ticket to the state capital. So don't fuck with me," Ellen said.

"Calm down, Ellen. The murders are putting a bit of an unwelcome light on our fair little town, as you know. That new editor at the *Herald*—Declan O'Brien—is snooping around every corner in town. He's milking this story for everything it's worth. For my money, it was probably some robbery gone bad. It'll die down soon and we'll sell those final parcels. Everyone in the partnership will make out fine," George said calmly.

"O'Brien isn't going to uncover my stake in the partnership, is he George?"

"You're well protected on that score, Ellen. Don't lose any sleep over it."

"Are you losing any sleep over it?

"I get a good night's sleep every night. What have you heard about the police investigation?"

"I just spoke with Detective Morrissey this morning. They were able to get some boot prints and tire tracks from the scene. They're trying to trace them. Not much else. The fire took care of that."

"What about that other woman who was killed?"

"If it doesn't relate to the Placid development. I don't care. It's tragic that a little girl lost her mother, of course. But it looks to me like some kind of lovers' quarrel. You know how love affairs can go sour."

"Yep, I see them all the time on TV."

"So have you spoken with the son. What's his name?"

"Caleb Reynolds. Yes, we're getting together after the funeral. It wouldn't be right to talk to him about business before then."

"Of course. Just take care of it George, and quietly."

"We'll be back on track before the holiday. I guarantee it."

"That's what I like to hear, George. Have you ever thought

about moving to the state capital?" Ellen said as she leaned back in her chair and crossed her long legs slowly.

CHAPTER 19

Rock songs from the 1980s played softly on the old stereo system that was perched on a board near the ceiling of the White Stag, a neighborhood bar a few blocks down the hill from St. Thomas Aquinas church.

The establishment was half filled on a Friday night—mostly with locals who were recapping their week to one another over a light beer or watching a game on the small-screen TV. Declan had always like the White Stag because it was common and unpretentious. The owner had not yet succumbed to the need to install a gargantuan television on the wall. A reliable and modest color set that had respectable reception was enough for the crowd at the White Stag.

Declan and Father Joe shared a frozen pizza and a pitcher of beer at a corner table. Joe had exchanged his clerical clothes for jeans and a sweater. He was one of the regulars at the White Stag. His only rule for the patrons was not to ask him to hear their confession after they had imbibed too heartily.

"This weather reminds me of that winter when we were ten years old and went trudging through the snow to that abandoned quarry near your house, " Declan said.

"Who's idea was that anyway?" Joe said.

"I believe it was yours. You were always the leader. I guess I should have known that you'd be leading a flock some day," Declan said.

"And there was a time when you were always ready to follow. And that day I'm glad you did," Joe said.

"Maybe that was the day you heard God call you to service rather than the lightning strike on the golf course," Declan said.

"I don't think so. A ten-year-old boy wouldn't have the sophistication to see divine workings in the fact that his best friend grabbed him before he slid off a ledge into the quarry pit. I was grateful and a little scared, but not called to the priesthood that day," Joe said as he grabbed another piece of pizza. "I think I was more concerned about how to explain the rip in my pants to my mother."

"You know, Joe, I've got to tell you that I feel more comfortable talking to you in a setting like this than in a rectory. After all of these years, it's hard for me to be fully comfortable with the fact that you're a priest," Declan. "These stories just remind me that you were just a regular guy—you know, normal."

"And you see me as abnormal now?" Joe said.

"A little, yes. For an average person, much less someone like me who has, shall we say, strayed from the mother church, it's difficult to understand the strength of a spiritual calling. Most people just want to do something in their lives that's not boring and pay the mortgage," Declan said.

"And it's my calling to let those people know that there's more to life than the things you just described," Joe said.

"I guess I don't have the faith anymore. I can't believe in something beyond my physical surroundings. Of course, I know all of the arguments. Like why not believe in case there is something— a God maybe. But I'm comfortable in my non-belief, I guess. I would be more confused constantly fighting the internal battle of belief versus disbelief. I've sided with atheism and I'm happy with the choice," Declan said.

"Then I'm not going to try to convince you otherwise. I'd be wasting my time and yours," Joe said.

"But isn't that your job? To try to make me a believer?"

"My job is to spread God's word to those who are willing to accept it. I don't get extra bonus points from the cardinal for a target number of conversions per quarter," Joe said.

"That's comforting. Besides, the White Stag might not be

the optimal location for redeeming a lost soul, particularly with Foreigner playing on the stereo," Declan said.

"So, let me ask you a more secular question, Declan," Joe said. "Do you want to get remarried someday?"

"It's too soon to think about such things. I felt burned by Kate. But I did have lunch with Nora Morrissey a few days ago. That's the closest thing to a confession you'll be getting out of me tonight," Declan said.

"How is Nora?"

"Still beautiful."

"And still married."

"That, too. I just wanted to talk to her again. It was all very proper, Father. Don't you miss looking at women, you know, in that way?"

"Of course I find women attractive. I just cannot act on it. I have many women friends. I just keep the relationships on an intellectual or spiritual level," Joe said.

"Is it hard?"

"It's my vow."

"Well, don't worry, I won't be a home wrecker."

"That's good to know, Declan. Let's have one more for the road. I've got to get back," Joe said. "I have an appointment—prenuptial counseling."

"OK. Finish up that last piece of pizza. Wasting food is a sin, you know," Declan said.

"It's good to know that even a heathen can recognize sin when he sees it. I don't suppose that I'll see you at Christmas midnight mass," Joe said.

"You'll see Moira, but not me. I wish I were in Hawaii or someplace exotic this time of year--away from all of the consumer hassle and the phony sentiment."

"A refuge from all that is exactly what you'll find in church."

"Nice try, Joe. Eat up. You have an impressionable young couple to counsel, remember. I'm not that easily converted."

When Declan returned home, he replayed in his head many of the things that Joe had said about the religious life. For him, he concluded, the largest barrier was the implied obligation that to believe in a god meant being part of a larger religious community. He did not want to feel that engaged, that connected. As he drifted off the sleep he also determined that Joe looked very comfortable and normal in secular clothes. He looked like he had always remembered him.

CHAPTER 20

Nora felt a pang of guilt talking to Christa Bennington's former lover—Roone Hutton—the day after her funeral, but Christa's sister Allison had directed Nora's attention to him. In a phone conversation with Allison, Nora learned that Christa and Roone had been involved for three years before Christa had moved back to Lacroix, and that the relationship continued off and on during Christa's first year in town.

Roone sat stoically in one of the police station's interview rooms. Nora's eyes were drawn to his teeth, which sparkled like ice on a cold January day. His fingers were manicured and his hair was standing up awkwardly because of the static in the dry air. Roone Sutton, the eldest son of a New York real estate developer, owned a successful art gallery in New York City's SoHo neighborhood. He looked uncomfortable, Nora thought. But she wondered whether it was caused by the tragedy of Christa's death, being out of New York City or guilt.

"Thank you for coming by this morning, Mr. Sutton. I appreciate it," Nora said. "And please accept my condolences."

"Thanks, detective. I'll do anything I can to help the police find Christa's killer, " Roone said.

"What was the exact nature of your relationship with Christa?"

"We were friends. And before that lovers. But I suppose you know that already," Roone said.

"Are you the father of Christa's daughter?"

"No. Absolutely not."

"Her sister Allison thinks that you might be."

"She's wrong."

"But you were still seeing her after she moved here?"

"Yes. But it wasn't like it used to be. It used to be exciting. Electric, you know. But Christa changed when her mother became ill and she moved back here. I'm a New Yorker. A big city guy. We grew apart. Even though we still kept in touch and I would visit her occasionally."

"Is it possible that you could be the father and Christa didn't want to tell you because she didn't want you in her child's life?"

"I told you. I'm not the father. I asked the question myself three years ago when Christa said she was pregnant. Christa assured me that it definitely wasn't mine," he said, growing annoyed at Nora's line of questioning. "In fact, when she said it she sounded relieved that it wasn't mine. But Christa wouldn't tell me or apparently anyone else who the father is, not even her own sister. She could be very secretive. That was her way. Mysterious and aloof Christa. Or maybe she was just ashamed."

"So Christa cheated on you?"

"Yes. I guess you could say that."

"How did that make you feel?"

"I was angry and upset, of course. How do you think I felt? She got herself pregnant by an anonymous rustic here in Lacroix. It's so…disappointing."

"Did you ever get over your anger?"

"Just ask me what I think you're going to ask."

"Where were you last Tuesday night?"

"In New York, of course. Check my phone records. Check my credit card receipts. Flight manifests, whatever. All of the things that they do on cop shows. Do whatever the fuck you want. I wasn't here. I didn't kill her."

"Where exactly in New York were you?"

"I was with a group of friends, including my girlfriend Sophie, at dinner at a restaurant called Images. It's in the art gallery district. I paid the bill."

"So you have a new girlfriend and you paid the bill. How gallant."

"Such sarcasm doesn't become you, Detective Morrissey."

Nora wanted to joust with him more on this topic, but decided that he would enjoy it too much. She would check his alibi. But she sensed that he was telling the truth—at least about not killing Christa himself.

"Do you know who might have killed her?"

"No. I was her friend, but she lived in a different world."

"When was the last time you saw Christa and Paris?"

"I was here for a weekend in July. We went to some lakeside cabin in Wisconsin. Christa and Paris both like the beach. I was bored, but I enjoyed their company. Too many trees and bugs up there for me. I prefer concrete and fine wine."

"How often did you and Christa talk?"

"About once a month I would say."

"Did she know about Sophie?"

"Yes, she was happy for me. New Yorkers are sophisticated about these things."

Nora refused to take the bait. "Did Christa seem normal to you? She didn't mention anything about feeling scared or threatened by anyone?"

"No. She seemed very content. She was looking forward to the holidays. It was hard for me to believe or understand, but she really liked it here."

"Many people do, Mr. Hutton."

Roone did not respond.

"That's all of the questions I have for now. If anything else comes up, I'll be in touch," Nora said.

"Nothing else will come up," Roone said as he put on a leather jacket that was chic but too light for a December day in Lacroix.

"What kind of art do you sell in your gallery, Mr. Sutton?"

"Are you an art lover?"

"A little."

"Our gallery sells a mix of modern and contemporary works—from Pollack to Rosencrantz."

"Rosencrantz?"

"He's really hot right now. A great artist. I discovered him, I'm pleased to say. His colors and shapes are sarcastic but grand."

"What about Thomas Conrad?"

"He paints crap for suburban housewives who don't travel enough. Please don't waste your money, detective, if you are thinking of buying one of his paintings."

"No, I wasn't planning to, but thanks for your critique. I'll keep that in mind."

When Nora returned to her desk, there was a package waiting for her. She opened it and found a calendar featuring a different French country scene for each month and a compact disc of Darius Milhaud's *Suite Provençale*. The card was from Declan, who wrote: "Bon voyage. Here's a little touch of warm Provence in the winter."

CHAPTER 21

Declan didn't like Christmas. He found the season filled with too many pained rituals, obligatory observances and social pressures that were empty of meaning for him. His attitude didn't arise only from adult cynicism. He began to detest the holiday since he was a child. His parents invited over relatives with whom he had nothing in common but with whom he had to engage in tortured friendliness. "It won't hurt you to be nice to your cousins once a year," his mother would say. But Declan never had a heightened sense of familial obligation. Just because people are related to you, he always thought, does not make them nice or interesting to be with.

Since that time of strained conversations and attempts to keep his toys from being broken by his rough-housing cousins, he always associated the holidays with being forced to spend time with people who always had the same opinions about the same things and who never seemed to change except for their ages. And he resented being dragged year after year to midnight mass. He thought that there could be few evenings colder than those nights when parishioners plodded to church at midnight in the dead of winter. He would rather be cross-country skiing in Antarctica.

Now he was back in a place where Christmas was revered. But he had learned long ago to keep his mouth shut about his holiday perspective. As he left his house to have Christmas dinner with sister Moira and her family, he engaged in his latest holiday sidestep with his neighbor Edith Pregler, who was returning from walking her Scottish terrier Eddie.

"Merry Christmas, Declan. I was looking for you at mass last night," Edith said.

"Merry Christmas, Mrs. Pregler. I wasn't feeling well, so I just decided to stay home where it was warm. It's still pretty cold today. You and Eddie shouldn't stay out here long," he replied.

"Oh, no. We're heading back in. I see you have some presents. Going to Moira's?" she asked.

"Yes," Declan said as he moved to his car.

"It's good that you and Moira still have each other since the passing of your parents, God rest their souls. What a waste. You be sure to wish Moira a Merry Christmas for me, and tell her to stop by one of these days."

Maneuvering to avoid a prolonged reminiscence with Mrs. Pregler about his parents, Declan decided to enter his car and start the engine. From the front seat he responded: "I will, Mrs. Pregler. Well, I have to be going or I'll be late."

Declan backed his car out of the driveway and headed to the new subdivision called Sussex Estates where Moira and her husband Tommy had recently purchased a house for themselves and their two children Patrick and Emily—ages twelve and ten. The house had huge picture windows and numerous vaulted ceilings. After seeing it for the first time, Declan thought that it looked more like a suburban church than a private residence. But he hadn't been in too many churches that boasted a hot tub and a gigantic flat screen television. Their housing choice notwithstanding, he liked Moira's husband and her children because they at least acknowledged a world outside of Lacroix. Summers spent at his family's cabin in northern Michigan were a more enlightened choice than never leaving Lacoix at all.

This was the first time in many years, however, when he would be spending a holiday with them. While married to Kate, Declan usually spent the holidays with her parents in exotic locales—like Hawaii or a hunting lodge in the Scottish Highlands. This would be the first Christmas that he and Moira would be spending together without their parents. Declan hoped that the day would not become a slow dance into tearful childhood reminiscences.

Bright sunlight reflected off the snow and shot through his

windshield like a bullet. He looked like a turtle as his head stuck out of his red parka that he had purchased in Fairbanks, Alaska during a hiking trip. The streets of Sussex Estates were nearly deserted as he pulled into the cul-de-sac where his sister lived.

Declan was greeted warmly by his sister and his niece and nephew. His brother-in-law Tommy was in the kitchen carving the turkey. The house dripped with Christmas cheer, a sharp contrast to Declan's home where there was no sign of the holidays save for the Christmas cards he placed on the fireplace mantel.

Christmas dinner progressed as Christmas dinners usually do, with the requisite updating of personal details amidst the over indulgence of food. Declan learned about Patrick's basketball practice and Emily's gymnastics and piano lessons. He learned that Tommy's certified public accountant practice was booming, and that the busy tax preparation season was just beginning. But Tommy said that he still made time to go pheasant and deer hunting with his brother Matt. Over the years, Declan had politely declined to join them, not because of any moral position about hunting but because he instinctively knew that he would not be good at it. He did not want to spend cold mornings apologizing for his hunting ineptitude.

Moira explained that she was planning to redecorate the kitchen, even though the house was less than one year old. Declan contributed stories about his new job at the *Lacroix Herald* and explained that there was nothing new to report about the Reynolds or Bennington murders. The tenor of the conversation was what Declan referred to as the comforting reassurance of the mundane and familiar. But he was always looking for that unique experience that his father had always taught him to seek. "Look for the thing that broadens your horizons," he would tell Declan.

Declan's mind drifted to where he had been last Christmas. He spent the holiday with Kate and her family in Maui soaking in the tropical warmth and hiking in the crater of the dormant volcano Haleakala. It would be their last Christmas together, although he didn't know it at the time. As he sat in front of the fire observing

Patrick and Emily playing with their new toys, Declan thought of the clouds rolling into the crater from the ocean, creating a white blanket beneath the dazzling blue sky above it. And he recalled the immense silence of the landscape that looks like Mars. It was a Dantean paradise and purgatory rolled into one. It was a place where the sun burned you and the wind chilled you at the same time.

It was the same sensation on the skin that Declan remembered as a child when he and his best friend Joe set fire to cardboard boxes in the woods in the middle of winter. It was probably fifteen degrees below zero. Near the roaring fire, their skin nearly burned. If they stepped just a few feet away, they began to freeze. To Declan, it was a seductive opposition. Declan and Joe stayed in the woods until the fire burned itself out and it became too cold to remain. Their clothes smelled of smoke. Their mothers were angry with them both.

Before leaving his sister's, Declan dutifully conveyed Mrs. Pregler's request that Moira visit her. He knew that Moira would do so. Moira was dependable in that way. He managed to avoid another encounter with Mrs. Pregler and Eddie when he returned home. Melville was sleeping. Declan turned up the heat and chose a collection of Spanish guitar music to help him fall asleep.

CHAPTER 22

After a few weeks at Howl making more money than she ever had before, Teresa bought herself a used car so that she and her mother would no longer have to share one. Teresa had now stopped working with her mother, who now handled her cleaning clients by herself. To make it up to her mother, Teresa began buying nicer furniture for their small apartment and more fashionable clothes for herself. "By the end of the year, we'll be moving out of this place," Teresa promised her mother. Anna had recently told her that she was moving out at the end of the month. Anna and her boyfriend Carl Holstrom had bought a townhouse together in the new development called River Bluff Park.

Maria still did not approve of the place in which Teresa worked, but she did not complain about the clear upswing in their financial position and material surroundings. But she prayed for her daughter every night. She still had her faith.

Teresa learned to deal with the leers and the gropes of the more inebriated patrons at Howl. Sometimes she laughed off the unwanted advances, and at other times she made certain that the man or men were removed. Hal reminded all of the women who worked at Howl that if customer wanted a feel they had to pay.

Teresa discovered that the waitresses and strippers who worked at Howl were a varied group. Serena used to be a star high school gymnastics star in Minnesota. Eileen was a divorced mother of a two-year-old girl. Shelley spent six months in jail for shoplifting. Audrey dropped out of college for a year because her finances ran low and she wanted a job that paid more than a fast food joint so that she could return to finish her degree next year. And then there was Anna, the clear superstar at Howl whom all the men wanted to meet in the VIP room. Whatever she was doing, Teresa thought, she was making enough to buy herself a townhouse.

Teresa visited Anna a few days before she moved out. Anna was busily packing boxes and throwing out old things that she didn't want in her new home.

"Carl and I want a fresh start. Our place in River Bluff Park is beautiful. You'll have to see it," Anna said.

Teresa had never met Carl. Anna always stayed at his place. All Anna told her was that he was an electrician and a handyman and that they did not meet at Howl.

"Anna, Carl doesn't have a problem with what you do at Howl?"

"Why should he? My money is paying for our place as much as his. Besides, Carl's a nice guy. He doesn't have a problem that I'm with other man as long as I come home to him at the end of the night. What I do at Howl and other places is business. That's all, just business. What I do with Carl is pleasure. And I do mean pleasure. Carl's got a horse cock, if you know what I mean," Anna said.

"What other places do you mean?" Teresa asked. Teresa avoided engaging Anna in discussions about sex or using slang terms for the act. It's not that Teresa didn't enjoy sex. She just preferred not to talk about it like people talk about sports and what kind of food they ate. Sex was a private activity that Teresa preferred to keep private.

"What's goes on in the VIP room is tame. It's a few naked lap dances and maybe a blow job in the bathroom, but nothing more than that. Things get really freaky and more lucrative at private parties at those big houses on the west side of town or at the fancy River Queen Hotel downtown. I have few regulars who treat me well," Anna explained.

"I don't know if I could do that, with all of those different men. Stripping is one thing that I might consider. God knows that Hal's asked me enough times. But, Anna, I don't know. Aren't you frightened of what might happen?" Teresa said.

"Shit no. I know how to take care of myself and I'm not into anything violent, like bondage or spanking, you know. Most of these guys just want a little excitement that they can't find elsewhere. I think they're all married, but I don't really ask. It's not professional. But that's the feeling that I get. You know one regular asked about you a few night ago," Anna said.

"What do you mean?"

"I've told you before. You've got these sexy Mediterranean looks, not the bottle blond thing like most of the ladies there. Men think you're one exotic bitch. Do you want to meet him?"

"So he can screw me? I don't think so."

"Are you getting any from somebody else? You told me you hadn't had a boyfriend since you cam here from Chicago. You must be really ready. So why not make some money doing it? You don't have to fuck him at first. Tell him that you'll just strip or play with yourself. Get to know him. See what he's like. He's a pretty distinguished guy. And he pays really well. But you have to keep your mouth shut. He insists on that. He demands that you be discreet. That's no problem for me, with the money he's willing to shell out."

"I don't think so, Anna. I'm fine with the tips that I get serving drinks."

"You'll get tired of that soon enough. That's the bottom of the ladder at a place like Howl. You just get scraps compared to the other girls. You got a lot going for you. Use it, "Anna said.

"I don't know."

"I think you do know. You just have to convince yourself that you're willing to leverage your assets. I read that in one of those investment magazines that Carl has lying around. Honey, you've got the market cornered on the hot Latina babe stuff. It would be a terrible thing to waste. Anyway, can you get me another box from the kitchen? I'm almost done packing. Good riddance to this fucking dump."

CHAPTER 23

Nora sat on the sofa of her family room that was illuminated by the red and green Christmas tree lights. It was three o'clock in the morning. Randy and the kids were sleeping. A few stray scraps of wrapping paper lay on the carpet next to gifts that had been ripped opened a few hours ago.

Nora looked at the necklace that Randy had given her. It was expensive and beautiful, she thought. Randy was not cheap. But it was just another thing amidst the many other expensive things that they had accumulated over the years. She wondered if the little girl of Christa Bennington was crying for her mother tonight. She wondered what the sons and daughters and grandchildren of Judd and Miriam Reynolds were feeling when they sat around the dinner table and looked at the empty spaces where the family matron and patron had once sat, said grace, carved the turkey and laughed.

She felt like she was failing the families of the victims. There were no hard clues in either case. She still held suspicions about Christa's ex-lover Roone, but his alibis all checked out. And there were only some boot prints and tire tracks at the Reynolds farm that could lead to hundreds of possible suspects and hundreds of dead ends.

She played the French music CD that Declan had sent. She turned the volume low so that she would not wake her family. She closed her eyes and tried to imagine the dazzling wheat fields and delicious blue skies of southern France.

She leaned over to the phone and began dialing Declan's number. She stopped before it rang. Then she dialed again until Declan picked up.

"Yes. Who is it?" Declan said as he struggled to emerge from a deep sleep.

"Declan, it's Nora. I'm sorry to call you so late. I'm surprised that you answered."

"I always answer in the middle of the night. It's usually something terrible or tragic, so I don't want to hear about it on an answering machine. Are you going to tell me something awful?"

"No. I've just been sitting hear thinking about the murders and wondering if I have the skill to solve them, " she said.

"Some good Catholic self doubt never hurt anyway. Pride goeth before the fall, remember," Declan said.

"Please, Mr. Atheist, don't go biblical on me," Nora said. "I do have a proposition for you, though. I know that this probably overturns all the police regulations and procedures, but I just have this feeling that we can solve these crimes by working together, in secret. I do some digging and share some information with you, and you reciprocate. You could talk to some people without spooking them. Tell them that your sources will remain confidential."

"I don't know. My job is to report the news, not help solve crimes. And you have officers on the force to help you."

"The only other detective is off on medical leave. And as for the other officers, well, let's just say they do an adequate job of giving tickets."

"What about some help from the state or the FBI? These are high-profile cases."

"I could try those avenues, but I don't want to. I'm giving you the chance to be on the inside of a police murder investigation. And, frankly, I think I'll need all the help that I can get, especially from someone whom I can trust."

"The investigations have stalled?"

"I'm following leads and getting tips, but nothing solid."

"What does that say to you?"

"What do you mean?"

"I mean that Lacroix is not a big town. While it's a quaint cliché to think that everyone knows everybody else in Lacroix, it's still true that this town isn't Chicago or Detroit where someone can just disappear into one of a thousand different neighborhoods. If it were some robbery or drug-induced killings, I'd think you could dig up some suspects fairly quick. But you haven't. You're stuck. That in itself should lead you down some different paths."

"You think there's something exceptionally insidious about these crimes?"

"Yes, I think so. Definitely. I smell a big story here. But then again, I could be totally off the mark and might be smelling some conspiracy when there is none."

"So will you help me find out if there is anything rotten in Lacroix?"

"Making Shakesperean allusions at, what time is it, after three in the morning? That's pretty impressive, Nora."

"I went to college, too, Declan."

"Of course. Look, I hate to cut this conversation short, but I have an interview with Mayor Norberg early tomorrow morning," Declan said.

"About what?"

"About the Placid development and her thoughts on where Lacroix is heading in the coming new year."

"Sounds gripping."

"It pays the bills."

"So you'll help? We'll be in touch?"

"I think we can both gain from this alliance, Nora."

"Good. If you had declined I would have asked one of the patrolmen to give you a ticket on some trumped up moving violation."

"I'm glad that you had a contingency plan in place. Good night, Nora."

"Good night, Declan."

Declan rolled over on his back and his cat Melville returned to his place on Declan's stomach. Nora turned off the Christmas tree and music and went back upstairs. She could hear Randy snoring before she opened the bedroom door.

CHAPTER 24

"The Placid development is one of the key pieces—if not *the* key piece—to Lacroix's future development. It will mean jobs and an improved tax base for the city. And it will also attract new and different businesses to Lacroix. I would even go so far as to say that the Placid development signals a renaissance in our community. I applaud the vision of Thomas Conrad and the hard work of his partners in making the development a reality," Ellen Norberg said to Declan O'Brien, who was taking notes to accompany the tape recording he was making of the interview.

"But how many people in Lacroix will really benefit from the development, Mayor Norberg? From what I've seen, the development will be like an entirely separate town, not integrated with the rest of Lacroix," Declan said.

"A rising tide raises all boats. I firmly believe that. Look, Lacroix's economic past was based on farming and light industry. Both sectors have been fading for years. Do the citizens of Lacroix want to live in a town that continuously decays and shrinks, or live in a town that takes advantage of the natural beauty of the river and bluffs and the surrounding rural splendor? I think the answer is clearly the latter. In the past, the land was there to grow crops. Now the land is there to nurture serene lifestyles. I think that in five or ten years, Lacroix will become the Martha's Vineyard or Aspen of the midwest. That's a positive outlook," Ellen said.

"But positive for whom? You really didn't answer my question."

"I believe I did. If we attract people with money and capital, they will create new jobs. I concede that the jobs might be different, but they are jobs nonetheless."

Declan thought of former farmers or assembly-line workers stacking shelves in superstores or running cash registers in upscale boutiques. He thought of the blue collar workers who need food handouts from the local churches.

"Do you think that the authentic nature of the town will change?" Declan said.

"Who's to say what authentic is or is not. That word changes over time. I'm more concerned with the current and future impression people have of Lacroix. I want Lacroix to be thought of as a refuge from many of the problems that plague urban areas. That's what the Placid development strives for. And I want to point out that there are other development efforts going on, like the riverfront reclamation with its townhouses and promenade."

"Then it's just a coincidence that three people were killed during this new era in Lacroix? Don't you think that these crimes undercut the image that you and others are trying to promote?"

"No. These crimes are horrible. There's no question about that. But I'm confident that our police department will solve them and that the killers will be brought to justice. I think reasonable people, however, will not hold these crimes against Lacroix. People are still buying houses and investing in Lacroix's future. The coming new year will be a bright one for our community. I'm confident of that."

"Do you have any political aspirations beyond being mayor of Lacroix?"

"Not at this time. But in politics, it's better never to say never, of course. My husband and I are happy here. It's our home town. Where we raised our children. I want to see firsthand Lacroix flower again," Ellen said.

"Well, Mayor Norberg, I think I've covered everything. We plan on running this piece in our new year's edition. Thank you again for your time," Declan said.

"If there's any thing else you need, please check with my assistant," Ellen said.

After Declan departed, Ellen called George Udelhoven.

"George, what do you know about Declan O'Brien?"

"I know that he's been snooping around various city departments looking for public records relating to Placid. And he's been trying to talk to people on my staff," George explained.

"Are they talking?"

"I don't think that they'd be stupid enough to do that. They've all got mortgages to pay."

"Good. Keep it that way. He was just in here interviewing me. I didn't like the tone of some of his questions. Keep an eye on him."

"I can do that."

"We don't want some local hack derailing our plans."

"It won't come to that, Ellen. The Placid lots are selling nicely and I'm making progress with Caleb Reynolds on his parents' land. By this time next year, Placid will have risen from the corn and soy fields. And we will all begin to harvest the benefits."

"By this time next year I expect to be sitting in the state legislature."

"You've got my vote," George said, trying to lighten the conversation with some humor.

"Just do your fucking job," Ellen replied. "I'll worry about getting votes."

CHAPTER 25

The choral finale of Beethoven's Ninth Symphony echoed gloriously throughout Alan Harrison's candlelit livingroom. Alan could see through a small opening in the heavily draped windows that it had began snowing again. He heard a car crunch on the fresh snow in the street.

"Keep fucking me faster, harder," Ellen said. She was bent over the back of Alan's large sofa that faced the fireplace. Alan had entered her from behind. He began thrusting faster and faster as Beethoven's tempo accelerated.

"Oh, yes. That's the way I like to be fucked," Ellen screamed as she dug her nails into one of the large pillows on the sofa. Alan could feel the sofa begin to slide forward across the antique oriental rug as he leaned his entire body toward Ellen. Ellen shuddered as he came inside her. He cupped her breasts in his hands. He inhaled the fragrance of her hair.

"Another fine performance, maestro," Ellen said a few minutes later after she had washed her face and put on the silk robe that Alan had given her for Christmas. She sipped a glass of wine while leaning against Alan on the sofa.

"The audience was quite appreciative," Alan responded.

"There's a slight problem that we need to discuss. Something that I'd like you to help me with," Ellen said.

"Of course. What is it?"

"Declan O'Brien. He's the city editor at the *Lacroix Herald*. He's been trying to dig up stuff about the financing of the Placid development," Ellen explained.

"I thought you said every one was protected. That George had been very careful," Alan said.

"No one is perfect. If someone looks long enough and hard enough and gets to the right person, they might find something. So we need to divert O'Brien's attention," Ellen said.

"What can I do?"

"It just so happens that O'Brien lives just a few blocks from here. I'd like you to create a distraction."

"I'm not following you, Ellen."

"Go over there tonight and start a fire at his house. And leave a note that simply says: "Leave Christa alone." Tonight's perfect. The snow will cover up any footprints. And hardly anyone is outside," Ellen said.

"Ellen, that's arson. Are you crazy? The house could burn down. He could be killed," Alan said, rising from the sofa and standing naked in front of the fireplace. "And the note is too melodramatic."

"Don't worry. He's not married and he doesn't have any kids. So there won't be any innocent victims. And, besides, I just want you to start a small fire near the back porch. The note will make him think that he's touching some nerves in the paper's reporting about the Bennington murder. Of course, that will make him dig even harder on this story at the expense of Placid. "

"I see your twisted logic. But the fire could spread. I won't do it, Ellen."

"I think you will, Alan. You'll do it for me."

"And what will the fire accomplish anyway?"

"O'Brien will also be receiving a message that will give him something to think about."

"Oh, great. We're threatening him as well. I don't want any part of it. This is just crazy."

"No, Alan, what's crazy is your refusal. Suppose university officials learned about your dalliances with those two undergraduate girls. And your discounted sweetheart investment in Placid. You want to get out of Lacroix as much as I do. But I hold your ticket. You can't go anywhere without me. Just take a deep breath and think about that, Alan."

Alan turned his back on Ellen and leaned against the fireplace mantel. The heat from the fire rose up and clutched his chest.

FIRE AND ICE

"Just a small fire, Ellen. That's all I'll do."

"Of course. I don't want anyone to get killed. Now shut up and come here," Ellen said as she reached out her hand to grab Alan's penis.

CHAPTER 26

Light snow was still falling from the storm the night before as Nora looked at the charred floorboards and railing of Declan's back porch.

"At first I thought it might have been some punk neighbor kids having some fun. Last night I could barely make out some footprints heading down the hill, but the snow has covered them up now," Declan said. "But then I found this note taped on my back door: "Leave Christa alone."

"What have you found out about Christa?"

"That's the thing. Not much. I'm not having any luck talking to friends or neighbors here or back in New York. It's as if her child was the result of some kind of immaculate conception. I can't find evidence of any relationship since she broke up with Roone."

"I guess you rubbed some of her friends the wrong way."

"But I always thought I was so pleasant and charming."

Nora smiled. "Did you hear anything last night?"

"I heard someone trip on the garbage cans along the side of the house. That's why I was able to get downstairs so fast. When I looked out of the window, I didn't see anybody but I saw the smoke coming from the back of the house. I threw a few buckets of water on it, and it was put out," Declan said. "It won't take much to fix it."

"I spoke with your neighbors, and they didn't see or hear anything. Not even Mrs. Pregler. Declan, this obviously wasn't just a random prank. Last night it was snowing pretty hard. There wasn't much traffic on the streets. Someone had to make a concerted effort to set fire to your porch," Nora said. "Give me the names of the people you spoke to about Christa. I'll see if I can find anyone who feels strongly that you're trying to sully her memory."

"Fine."

"How about your work on the Reynolds murders? Any better luck there?"

"I spoke with Mayor Norberg recently. And I'm trying to get someone from the Placid development partnership to grant me an interview," Declan said.

"Why them?"

"Because the Reynolds' land borders the Placid development. Maybe it wasn't a robbery. There's no evidence of that," Declan said. "Maybe it has something to do with the development."

"But I think that it could have been robbery, and that the murder of the Reynolds is tied with the murder of Christa Bennington," Nora.

"How do you figure that?"

"I've been looking through the financial records and receipts of both the Reynoldses and Bennington. They both used the same electrician in the past few months. His name is Carl Holstrom. I'm going to drop in on Mr. Holstrom later this afternoon. Maybe you can help me do some background digging on Mr. Holstrom. But you never heard the name from me," Nora said.

"My lips are sealed," Declan said, knocking portions of the charred railing into the snow. "Maybe I can get Father Joe to help me repair the porch. He likes to do these kind of things."

"Really?"

"Oh, yes indeed. Joe loves to build things as much as he likes to play golf and save souls."

"Not your normal man of the cloth."

"That's how I can tolerate him," Declan said.

CHAPTER 27

Through the floor-to-ceiling windows at the back of Carl Holstrom's townhouse, Nora could see the frozen Mississippi River glistening in the sharp winter sun. Across the river, wooded bluffs rose from the river like fists that had punched through the earth's crust.

The townhouse's wooden floors gleamed. Except for a large flat-screen television and an equally large leather sofa that dominated the first-floor livingroom, most of the townhouse was empty. Packing boxes were stacked up against the walls. Nora noted that the TV and sofa were very expensive brands that her husband favored.

Nora sat across the dining room table from Carl, who wore jeans, cowboy boots and a Green Bay Packers sweatshirt and hat. He scratched the two-days' growth of beard on his chin and sipped a cup of coffee. Nora thought that his blue eyes and his slightly graying blond hair made him ruggedly charming, like someone from a 1950s western movie.

"Pardon the mess. My girlfriend and I haven't finished unpacking yet," Carl said.

"What's your girlfriend's name?" Nora asked as she took out a notepad.

"Anna Schmidt. She out shopping for stuff—at Target or Wal-Mart or some place like that."

"Where does she work?"

"At a bar called Howl across the river in Belleview."

"I know it," Nora said.

"I'm not sure how I can help you, Detective Morrissey," Carl said, scratching the back of his neck.

"I'll get straight to the point. You worked for both Judd Reynolds and Christa Bennington. Is that right?" Nora said.

"Yeah, sure. I did some electrical work for both of them. They both lived in old houses, and wiring in those places needs to be replaced and upgraded. You know, things like that," Carl said.

"How did they find you?"

"Through word of mouth. I know Judd's second son Jim. Did some work on his new house. One day he asks me to help out his Dad, who was getting on in years and couldn't fix things like he used to."

"What about Ms. Bennington?"

"Let me think. Oh, yeah, I was doing some work down the street from her place. At the Murphys. She was walking by one day with her kid and she asked me for my card. A few months later, I got a call. Did a couple of jobs for her," Carl explained.

"Did you have any problems with Judd Reynolds or Christa Bennington? Did they pay you on time? Were they satisfied with your work?"

"Of course they were. I do good work for a fair price. Like I said, I keep busy from word of mouth mostly. Got to have a good reputation to keep in business," Carl said.

"What about Nellie Osvalt?"

"What about her?" Carl said, turning his head to look out of the window.

"She called the police on you. Said that you were harassing her for money."

"Is that what this visit is all about? That lying bitch. We agreed on a certain job at a certain price, and I expect to be paid for my work."

"So as a good business man you threaten her at all hours of the night?"

"It wasn't like that."

"How was it, Carl? Tell me how it was?"

"There's nothing to tell. The bitch wouldn't pay me so I needed to get her attention."

"You didn't think a lawyer would have been better?"

"All lawyers are assholes. Besides, after a while I just let it drop."

"Only after you were nearly arrested."

"But I wasn't. So let's move on. I've got things to do around here as you can see."

"It seems you have a temper, Carl. You busted a guy up at a bar. Got probation for that. Your ex-wife placed a retraining order on you," Nora said.

"She was lying."

"Another lying bitch, Carl? Was Christa Bennington a bitch, too? Did she try to stiff you on some bill? Or did you try to come on to her, and she told you to go to hell."

"I don't know that you're talking about."

"What I'm talking about Carl is that you are the only connection between the deaths of Judd and Miriam Reynolds and Christa Bennington. You worked for both. You were in both houses on multiple occasions. And you have a temper when you think people are doing you wrong," Nora said, her voice rising.

"You think I killed them? That's just fucking nuts."

"Can you account for your whereabouts on December twenty-first and twenty-second?

"I was probably out drinking with my buddies."

"You'll have to do better than that, Carl. Do you have a shotgun?"

"Yeah. Upstairs. I haven't used it in a while."

"Then you won't mind if I take it with me."

"Be my guest."

"And I'd like to send a forensics team over to look through your clothes."

"Should I be calling a lawyer or something?"

"Lawyers are assholes, Carl. You said so yourself. If you do call a lawyer, well, I'll just figure that you do have something to hide. And then I'll be all over you, Carl. You can count on that," Nora said.

"Fine. Bring in your fucking team of whatever you called them. I didn't kill those people. I admit that I can lose my temper. But I would never do something like that. I'm not an idiot. I got a future. A girlfriend. This nice place. I would have to be really stupid," Carl said.

"Most criminals are, Carl. That's what keeps me in business," Nora said. "Before I go, write down the places where you were on the dates that I mentioned and the people who can corroborate that you were there,"

"Fine, give me the damn paper."

"How much did you pay for this place, Carl?"

"What?" Carl said, raising his head from the paper on which he was writing. "One hundred seventy-five thousand. Why do you want to know that?"

"I always like to know about real estate options in Lacroix. Nice view."

"Yeah, real nice," Carl said.

CHAPTER 28

The instructions passed along to Teresa by Anna at Howl were to go to Room 1252 of the River Queen Hotel at nine o'clock. Teresa had been vacillating all afternoon about whether she was ready to take this step. Every five minutes she had wanted to cancel the appointment. She told herself that good girls don't sell sex for money. That's not how she was raised. But the money sounded too good and Anna had reassured her that it would be safe.

She had had multiple fumbling and unsatisfying sexual encounters with three different boyfriends back in Chicago. She never could figure why so much energy was put into songs and books and music about the subject. To her, the experience was underwhelming. It didn't cause her great pain, joy or anguish. So she decided that it could at least generate some income. It would be one step toward financial freedom; one step farther away from the grinding tedium that ruled her life.

"Just give these guys what they want and they'll be happy. And you might enjoy it, too. I don't see you getting laid these days," Anna said.

Anna told Teresa to wear a low-cut black cocktail dress. Her client liked elegance and sophistication with an understated sexuality. Teresa needed to buy such a dress quickly.

"Think of it as just like another work uniform," Anna said.

The River Queen Hotel had recently been renovated to duplicate its past glory when it was one of the midwest's grand railroad hotels. The lobby featured soaring granite columns and thick red carpeting. A string quartet played Mozart in the corner, near the entrance to the casino that was modeled after the elegant gambling palaces in Monte Carlo rather than the more pedestrian establishments in Las Vegas or Atlantic City.

Teresa was trying not to breathe too heavily or draw attention to herself as she entered the elevator to go to her appointment on the twelfth floor. She knocked on the door. The man who answered was wearing a business suit. His collar was still buttoned. He smiled and led her into a suite. Teresa could see the corner of the bed through the door on the side of the room. Her client then unbuttoned the top button of his shirt and loosened his tie. She noticed that his nails were manicured. He spoke softly and asked her if she wanted a drink.

"No thanks," she whispered.

"I've noticed you at Howl and asked Anna about you," the man said.

"Yes, she told me."

"You're very beautiful."

"Thank you."

"I'm one of Anna's regular customers. Did she tell you that? She's a very exciting woman. She pleases me. Will you be able to please me, Teresa?"

"Yes."

"That's what I like to hear."

"Can we get the business part out of the way now?" Teresa said, remembering Anna's coaching.

"Of course. It was two hundred dollars, right?"

"Yes. Two hundred."

"Here you go, Teresa," the man said, handing her four fifty-dollar bills.

"What would you like me to do?"

"Take off your clothes right where you're standing and then crawl on your hands and knees over there to the window. Undress slowly, please."

Teresa did as she was told until she was completely naked. She thought that she would be cold, but instead she was sweating. She then got on her hands and knees and crawled across the room. The carpeting was rough against her skin.

FIRE AND ICE

The man said nothing. He stared at her quietly. "Now turn around and crawl back across the room to me," he said. "Keep your head down until I tell you to look up."

As she crawled away she could hear the man unzipping his pants. "Stop," the man said. "Now look up."

Teresa raised her head and saw the man's erect penis above her. She knew what she would be asked to do next. Teresa thought to herself that he probably had the whole thing choreographed in his head before she had arrived.

After he had finished, he went to the bathroom. Teresa got dressed and walked out of the bedroom into the main room of the suite. She noticed a business card on the table. She quickly put it in her purse. Before she left, her client gave her an extra fifty dollars and told her that he would be contacting her again. She had spent less than thirty minutes in the man's room and had made two hundred fifty dollars in cash for letting a strange man satisfy himself. She did not feel dirty or cheap. She couldn't say that she particularly enjoyed the experience sexually, but it wasn't completely repulsive either. It was just business, she told herself. She felt like an entrepreneur with a bright future.

In the elevator, she read the card: "Dr. Harry Norberg, Podiatrist."

CHAPTER 29

Nora sounded both excited and confused when she asked Declan if she could visit him after work. She told him that Christa's sister Allison had found some information in Christa's belongings that could be important to the case.

Declan had tea brewing and Spanish guitar music by Andres Segovia playing on the stereo when Nora arrived shortly after seven o'clock. She carried a small brown folder that she put down on the coffee table in the den. Melville rubbed himself against her leg and then went back to his favorite chair by the fireplace.

"You sounded excited on the phone. What's up?" Declan said.

"Allison found these in Christa's office desk. There are many pictures of her and Paris and Father Joe Knipfel," Nora said. "Take a look at these."

Declan quickly scanned about two dozen photos of the trio at Christa's home and beside a lake. They were posing in front of a Christmas tree, snow sledding, swimming and eating.

"So what. Everyone knows that Christa looked to Joe for spiritual counseling. And that he was often at her house doing some small carpentry jobs," Declan said, handing the photos back to Nora.

"You're not seeing it, Declan. These aren't just innocent pictures. They're like family photos. Like the kind I have in my photos albums. These are just like the ones I have with Randy, Alexandra and Jenna. Doesn't that strike you as somewhat odd?" Nora said.

"Not if Christa somehow viewed Joe as a father figure for Paris. After all, we still don't know who Paris's biological father is. Christa didn't want us to know. Maybe she had a one-night stand with some local good 'ol boy and was embarrassed about the whole thing, but she didn't want to have an abortion. And we know that she told the guy from New York with the silly name Roone that he wasn't the father. What better father figure to have for a little girl than a real father, if you know what I'm getting at," Declan said.

"I'm not convinced that it's so innocent as you think it is," Nora said.

"Oh, come on, Nora. You actually think that Joe Knipfel is the father of Christa Bennington's little girl?" Declan said. "He's a priest. And a pretty dedicated one."

"Priests have been known to sin, Declan. I know he's your friend, but it's something that I think we should explore. That I think you should explore, since you have a history with him," Nora said.

"Sure. I'll walk into his office and ask him if he screwed Christa Bennington and if they had a love child together."

"I'm sure that you'll be more tactful," Nora said.

"And you think that he killed her, too?" Declan asked.

"I don't know that. But he's now a suspect in my mind," Nora said. "If you just try to view this like a dispassionate reporter and look at this relationship between them, you might be able to consider it a possibility."

"That will be hard for me to do, Nora. We grew up together. He said mass at my parents' funeral. Anyway, what about that other guy, Carl Holstrom? You said that you found fingerprints and hair fiber in Christa's house that matched his, " Declan said.

"He was in her house and he met her. He admits it. He did some odd jobs for her. But we could find nothing in his house or on his clothing that ties him to the murder. And his alibi checks out. He was drinking with buddies the night of the murder. Over a dozen people place him at a bar called Tramps during the timeframe when Christa was murdered," Nora said. "And we know there was no break in. Christa likely knew her killer. "

"And Christa knew Joe."

"He knew her very well. Just talk to him. I trust you to approach him in the most appropriate way."

FIRE AND ICE

"Why don't you talk to him yourself in your capacity as the lead detective?"

"I don't want to embarrass him if I'm wrong. He's a priest after all. I want to give him some benefit of the doubt. I'd like to see how he reacts when you bring up the issue of the photos. Tell him that Christa's sister gave them to you and that you thought he might like to keep them, something like that. As a memento of Christa and Paris."

"I'd be lying to a priest."

"So you think you may be damned now? Come on Declan. Say an 'Our Father' and get over it. This priest—your friend—may be a killer. And he might have done it to cover up his relationship with Christa. I don't like saying the words anymore than you do. But if he did it or knows anything about it, he has a moral obligation to cleanse his soul."

"And you'd like me to be his confessor, is that it?"

"If he feels a need to confess anything."

"This makes my skin crawl."

"Murders can do that do a person. So you'll talk to him?"

"Yes," Declan said. "I'll see if he's available tomorrow. After all, what do priests do during the week anyway, especially when it's not golf season?"

"I know that this won't be easy for you," Nora said. Both she and Declan sat silently.

"To change the subject and break this awkward silence, I saw the inside of those new condos along the river. Carl Holstrom and his stripper girlfriend just bought one."

"Since when have you been so interested in real estate?"

"Since everyone else in this town seems to be real estate crazy with all of these housing developments."

"It's a brave new world for our once quaint little town, Nora. But I'll think I'll stay in this big old dinosaur of a house. It has character."

"Yes it does. I feel comfortable here, " Nora said.

CHAPTER 30

For weeks since the murders of Judd and Miriam Reynolds, Declan had been trying to talk to someone at George Udelhoven's real estate office. He was having no luck. People were afraid to talk. Declan grudgingly admired Udelhoven's ability to intimidate so many people in such a small town where there were so many intertwined friendships and family connections.

He was working late one evening, trying to write an article and looking at basketball scores on the internet. His phone rang at eight o'clock.

"I might have some information about the murder of the Reynolds. Information that you would fine useful," a woman's voice said.

"Who is this?" Declan said.

"It's better for both of us that you don't know. Let's say that I have some information from inside George Udelhoven's real estate operation. Are you still there?

"I'm here. I'm listening," Declan said.

"I work as a bookkeeper at the Placid Partnership."

"I've tried to speak with several people at your place but no one would talk," Declan.

"That's because Mr. Udelhoven said that we'd lose our jobs if we talked to you or anyone from the paper. He mentioned your name specifically."

"I'm honored. But then why this phone call? Don't you feel worried about losing your job?"

"Sometimes you just can't keep quiet forever. I was losing sleep. Feeling guilty. So guilty that I couldn't even say anything to a priest during confession. The last time I went, I just made stuff up. I didn't like the way I felt afterward."

"Just tell me what's on your mind. What do you know?"

"I found out that Carl Holstrom has a small stake in the Placid Partnership. About seventy-five thousand dollars worth. But he didn't pay full price like other investors. He got the shares at a fifty percent discount. And what's more, he and his stripper girlfriend just bought one of those new townhouses along the river,"

"That doesn't sound suspicious to me. It sounds downright American," Declan said. "People can buy townhouses and real estate if they want to. That's no crime. Why is this of any interest to you?"

"Because Carl and I were once involved, and I know that he likes getting down and dirty. Bend the rules to his advantage, you know."

"So is this some kind of jealous revenge?"

"No, that's bulllshit."

"Then tell me what it is."

"I know that Carl has worked for Mr. Udelhoven on something called 'special projects.' I've seen the paperwork. Carl ain't no rocket scientist. He can fix things. But what's so special about his work that it has to be called 'special'? That he gets paid fifty thousand dollars in just the past three months. Then he turns around and get shares of the Placid Partnership and buys some fancy house. Something's not right. Carl's involved in something. You can count on that. He's found some angle."

"What's his angle?" Declan said, growing weary of the conversation.

"Carl's a man that always had work but never had no money. He drank or gambled it away while we were together. Something ain't right here. I'm telling you straight."

"Maybe he's changed from when you knew him."

"People don't change that much. Not in this town. Look, you can use this information or not. But I'm telling you, it's weird that Carl is now so close to Mr. Udelhoven that he's doing special projects. He's a goddamn handy man. Mr. Undelhoven and Carl run in different circles, if you know what I mean. One's beer and shots and the other is fine wine. One is strip club and the other is country club. I've seen Carl go in and out of Mr. Udelhoven's office many times. Carl just winks at me and never says a word. That bastard. I can tell something's up. You just turn over a few stones and you'll find something growing."

"Thanks for the information. I'll have to think about this before I go digging around in someone's private life. But please leave me your number in case I have any further questions," Declan said.

"No. I'll be contacting you again." Then the woman hung up.

Declan sat at his desk staring out of the window at the cars passing by on Central Street. Their exhausts floated for a few seconds in the heavy winter air and then vanished. He needed to call Nora. This is the second time that Carl Holstrom's name had surfaced.

CHAPTER 31

Anna gave Teresa a glass of wine and started a fire in the fireplace in the den. Teresa was amazed by Anna and Carl's new townhouse. It was like a palace compared to the small apartment where she and her mother lived. The hardwood floors were beautiful and the kitchen appliances sparkled.

"This is fantastic, Anna," Teresa said.

"Thanks. Carl and I just love it," Anna said. "It really says that we're going places in this town. That we just won't settle for less like some other people do."

"But this place must be really expensive."

"Well, you know that I make pretty good money with my business. And Carl has really been doing well lately. The real estate guy who runs that fancy development outside of town has been giving him a lot of work," Anna said.

"What kind of work?"

"You know, construction type of stuff and some other special things. And he recommends Carl to people who need work done. It's good to have a trade that pays well. If you know what I mean, Teresa," Anna said, nudging Teresa in the arm. "So how have things been going? We don't get to talk like we used to."

"Fine. I have this one regular client," Teresa said.

"Does he ask you to do any weird shit?"

"No, not really. I mean, he does ask me to crawl on the floor. But that's it."

"Men can be such fucking animals. But other than that, is he nice to you?"

"Yeah, yeah I guess. I mean he always tips me well."

"So it's easier than you thought it would be?"

"Yes. It's just business, just like you said."

"How often do you see him?"

"About twice a week."

"That's pretty good money. Plus what you're making in regular tips at Howl. What are you saying to your mother?"

"Nothing, of course. She would die. I keep telling her to quit her job. But she won't. She says it's honest work and her customers like her work. But I can see how tired she gets every day," Teresa said. "I want to do better for her. I want to get us into a place like this, where we can lifts our heads high and become part of the community."

"You gotta have goals, Teresa. That's good. Having goals is what got me and Carl here."

"So are you two getting serious or something?"

"Fuck no. I ain't never getting married. Or if I do, it won't be to Carl. He's nice and all, especially in bed. But he's still just a laborer. I want to spend my life with a real professional. You know, a business owner or a doctor or somebody like that."

"Or maybe a podiatrist?" Teresa said.

"A what?"

"A podiatrist. I looked it up. Somebody who's a foot doctor."

"Yeah, I guess a foot doctor would do. But I was thinking more of a surgeon type," Anna said. "So where did you come across that fifty-dollar word: 'podiatrist'?"

"My regular client is a podiatrist. One of his business cards fell out of his jacket or someplace and I picked it up."

"So you know who this guy is?"

"Yeah."

"Tell me. Maybe I know him. It's a small town, honey."

"I'm not sure I should, Anna."

"Come on. It's Anna here you're talking to."

"OK. His name is Dr. Harry Norberg."

"You're shitting me!"

"No."

"That's the fucking husband of the town's mayor, Ellen

Norberg. The mayor's husband is getting some ass on the side. Now that's sweet. That's really sweet. Teresa, I don't want to tell you how to run your business, but you gotta take advantage of this. There are possibilities here," Anna said.

"Possibilities?"

"Great possibilities," Anna said. "Let's have another glass of wine and talk—girl to girl."

CHAPTER 32

Declan awakened before dawn, shaken from sleep by a dream. He was climbing a mountain in the Andes with Joe, who was taking the lead. He and Joe were roped together. As Joe neared the summit, he lost his grip and began to fall. Declan's safety line prevented him from plunging to his death, but Joe had been injured in the fall. His head was bleeding and he was not responding to Declan's calls. To Declan, Joe appeared dead. Joe's weight at the end of the rope was beginning to pull Declan off the mountain. So Declan cut the rope, and Joe plunged into an icy crevasse. As Declan scrambled down the mountain to save his own life, he could hear the cries of Joe—who was not dead—calling for help and praying for God's blessing. That's when Declan awoke.

He looked at his clock. It was four o'clock in the morning. The day before he had told one of his reporters that he wanted to conduct the interview with Joe about his parish's Loaves and Fishes food program for the low-income and unemployed residents of Lacroix who couldn't afford groceries. Joe told him that he would be grateful for the publicity. Declan did not tell him about his other intended line of questioning—about Christa Bennington.

Declan arrived at the rectory of St. Thomas Aquinas at nine in the morning. Joe was just finishing breakfast after having said seven o'clock mass.

"Do you want some coffee, Declan?" Joe said.

"No thanks. Do you get much of a crowd for these week day masses?" Declan asked.

"Oh, there are a few dozen regulars. Mainly retired folks who live in the neighborhood. It gives them comfort," Joe said. "Let's go into my office and talk about the Loaves and Fishes program, shall we."

Declan followed Joe down the hall and sat in an chair while Joe sat on a sofa. The morning sun slanted through the windows.

"So what would you like to know first? How the program started? The need in the community? Fire away," Joe said, eager to share his enthusiasm about this aspect of his ministry.

"Joe, I feel very awkward. I didn't sleep very well last night. I kept going over and over in my mind how I was going to talk to you today. I almost didn't come," Declan said.

"What's troubling you, Declan?"

"These," Declan said. He opened an envelope that contained the photos of Joe, Christa and Paris together. Joe looked at them silently and then returned them to Declan.

"What do you want to ask me about?" Joe said.

"Don't you even want to know from whom I got these photos?"

"It doesn't matter. I was there when they were taken," Joe responded. "I assume that the police or somebody found them in Christa's house."

"It was Allison. Christa's sister. She found them buried in a drawer. So tell me, Joe. I'm here as a friend. I'm here talking to you as a friend before the police talk to you. You know that they'll want to talk to you. That Detective Morrissey will want to talk to you," Declan said.

"What do those photos say to you, Declan?"

"I don't want to tell you what I think they say. You tell me. After all, you were there."

"Christa was a dear friend. A wonderful woman. She was trying to find her way in life during the mother's illness. She was a smart woman. A funny woman. A sophisticated woman. She was a woman and I am a man. And I sinned, Declan. I have sinned. In God's eyes I sinned. Maybe not in the secular world, but in my world. Frankly, I'm a bit relieved. I know that the day of judgement would come one day," Joe said. He directed his gaze out the window of his office.

"Are you Paris's father?"

"Yes, Joe. I am."

"Shit," Declan muttered. "Shit, Joe. This is bad, really bad. And Christa?"

"Over the past few months, we had more and more arguments. She wanted me to leave the priesthood and marry her. Be a real father to Paris. I told her that I couldn't do that. That being a priest was my true calling, my mission. Why couldn't we just keep things the way they were, I asked her. I begged her. But she insisted and insisted and she threatened and threatened."

"Threatened?"

"Threatened to expose me as her lover and Paris's father. That would destroy me, destroy my parish, destroy all of my work."

"So you did what, Joe? Tell me. Tell me how it happened."

"I went over to her house that night. And we fought like we had been fighting. I told her to keep her voice down because she would wake up Paris. I didn't want Paris to see us fighting. But she kept on screaming louder and louder. And I was getting angrier and more afraid. There was a hammer sitting on the coffee table. I don't know why the hammer was there. Maybe she was hanging some new pictures. I don't know. She never put things away in their proper place. That was one of her quirks. All I know is that I picked up the hammer. First, I just threatened her. She started to laugh and told me that I would never hurt her. She began taunting me. So I hit her, first on the shoulder. She cried out in pain and began to scream even louder. I hit her again and again to keep her quiet. I don't know how many times I hit her. But when I was finished she was on the floor and there was blood coming out of her head. I was ashamed at what I had done. Ashamed and afraid. So I took the hammer and left. I put the hammer and my clothes in the trash when I returned here."

"Then what did you do?"

"I walked and walked in the cold. My face began to freeze. I walked all the way to the river. I wanted to jump in, but it was frozen. So I just stood on the flood wall and I prayed to God for forgiveness, for some kind of sign as to what to do."

"Joe, you killed a woman. You killed a woman. You killed the mother of your child, for God's sake. And you have been keeping this inside of you for all of these weeks. You were just going to go on with your life," Declan said. "I can't fucking imagine. I can't imagine the torture. The sleepless nights. All of it."

"I'm a sinner, Declan. I deserved to feel guilty. Can you forgive me?"

"Will you stop saying that!" Declan said. "I can't forgive you."

"No, I guess you can't."

"You know what I have to do, don't you?"

"Of course, I know. I know that punishment is the consequence of my actions."

"I need to make a phone call. I need to call Nora Morrissey."

"Would you mind going out in the hall, Declan? I would like to be alone please."

"Sure, Joe. Sure," Joe arose and walked out into the hall to call Nora on his cell phone. From inside the office he could hear Joe crying.

CHAPTER 33

Declan waited alone in the rectory. Joe had asked if he could wait in the church and pray until Nora arrived. "Do whatever you have to do, Joe," Declan said.

Nora arrived at the church after about ten minutes. Officer Dave Henderson arrived in another car.

"Where is he, Declan?" Nora asked.

"He told me that he wanted to go into the church and pray," Declan explained.

"Now will you tell me what this is all about, Nora?" Officer Henderson said.

"Dave, we think Father Knipfel killed Christa Bennington. We're here to arrest him, " Nora explained.

"A priest? We're going to arrest a priest? That ain't right," he said.

"If it's any comfort, Dave, we all feel a bit awkward right now. So let's just do it, "Nora said.

Nora and Dave followed Declan through the rectory to the church. They expected to find Joe in silent prayer on the altar, but he was not there. The church was dark except for the light coming through the stained-glass windows that showed the signs of the cross.

"I thought you said he was going to be here," Nora said.

"That's what he told me," Declan said, not believing that Joe would run. "Joe! Joe, it's Nora Morrissey and Officer Henderson." His voiced echoed in the empty church.

"Joe, it's Nora. Don't make this any more difficult than it already is, " she said.

"Peace be with you, Nora, " Joe said. He was standing high above them in the back of the church in the choir loft. His voice echoed off the walls of the empty church.

"Joe, please come down. We're here to take you in so that you can explain your side of the story. There's always a story to tell, Joe," Nora said. "I'd like to hear it."

"This is some high school reunion, isn't it," Joe said, leaning against the railing of the choir stall. "There's you, Nora. You talked about joining the police force for as long as I can remember. And now there you are—a detective. And you Declan. Remember all of the time we spent together playing sports, playing golf, enjoying each other's company. Now look at us," Joe said.

"Just come down, Joe. This isn't the end of anything," Declan said.

"Oh yes it is, Declan. I'm a disgrace to my church, to my family, to myself. I thought I was given a sign to join the church on that day when lightning struck. But what if God wasn't telling me to become a priest? What if it was my own ego speaking? I've always been tormented. Tormented by other choices I could have made, other things I could have done with my life. But I kept them all to myself. I had to. My role was to comfort others, not to complain about my state," Joe said. "I want the torment to end. I loved Christa and Paris. I did. But it should have been a different kind of love. I have sinned."

Joe then climbed up on the railing and jumped from the choir loft to the pews below him. Declan would always remember the loud crack of Joe's body hitting the hard wood of the pews. It reminded him of a ball being struck by a bat. No one said anything as Joe plunged through the air. No one could believe it was happening.

They rushed to the back of the church. Blood streamed out of Joe's head and his arm was twisted behind him. His white collar was stained a deep crimson. Nora touched Joe's neck.

"He's dead," Nora said softly. "Call an ambulance, Dave."

"Shouldn't we say a prayer or something?" Dave said.

FIRE AND ICE

"Say it to yourself, Dave. It won't do Joe any good now," Nora said.

Declan could not stand there and gaze at his dead friend. He went back toward the altar, sat in the front row of pews and bowed his head.

Pain does not come at the moment of the initial shock. Pain comes later, at three o'clock in the morning when the only sound that you can hear is your own breathing and the walls of your house creaking. Later that day, Declan sat in the dark in the den of his house thinking about why it was so difficult to comprehend another human heart. He wanted to cry but he could not. He sat and stared at the patterns in the area rug on the wooden floor. He stared out of the window at the snow drifts in the street. He heard the rumble of a distant freight train. He couldn't believe that his friend Joe Knipfel would be joining his parents in the frozen ground.

CHAPTER 34

Teresa and Anna devised a plan for blackmailing Dr. Harry Norberg. Anna advised Teresa that the best way to get money out of him would be send an anonymous note to the mayor, telling her about her husband's infidelities. Teresa was worried that they would be the one who would be punished for their scheme.

"Don't worry, Teresa," Anna said. "There's nothing a politician hates more than being embarrassed by a scandal. They'll pay up. I can guarantee you that. I have some experience in these things. Trust me."

Anna helped Teresa write the letter to Mayor Norberg. And then they waited for the response.

The day the letter arrived at city hall Ellen Norberg was talking on the phone with George Udelhoven about the suicide of Father Knipfel and the resolution of the Bennington murder investigation.

"This is good news, George," Ellen said.

"How do you figure that?" George said.

"It tells people that there's not some lunatic murderer running around Lacroix. Bennington's murder was an isolated crime of passion. People can understand that. It could happen anywhere. And they'll soon forget about it."

"But the fact that it was a Catholic priest who fathered a child and murdered the child's mother brings out all kinds of media attention," George said.

"But the sensation of it all will soon be forgotten. We're all a nation of short-term enthusiasms, George. The TV news stories and the radio talk shows will move on to something else, and we can focus on getting the Placid development front and center again," Ellen said.

"Did you know Father Knipfel?"

"I probably met him once or twice. He ran a food program that I might have visited during a past election. I do remember that he was quite an athlete when he was younger. And he was quite good looking, for a priest. Well, at least not all priests are out molesting children. He seemed like a real man with typical desires," she said. "It's a shame he felt that he would rather die than face the shame of what he did."

"I guess so, Ellen," George said, wanting to change the subject of the conversation. "Speaking of appearances, remember the photo opportunity with Tom that's coming up. We're moving along on the construction of phase one homes at Placid and we want to get some publicity photos."

"It's on my calendar, George. I'll be there," Ellen said. She hung up the phone and began to open the special delivery package that her assistant had put on her desk. She read the letter several times before she called her husband Harry.

"Harry, it's Ellen. Meet me at home in an hour. We've got something to talk about."

"What?"

"Oh, just that you're a fucking idiot. And that we need to take care of this mess right away."

"I don't know what you mean, Ellen."

"Let me paint an image for you. Visualize that you're sticking your dick into some whore at the River Queen Hotel. Does this jog your memory?"

"I'll be home in an hour," Harry said.

"That should give you enough time to come up with some lame ass excuse," Ellen said.

CHAPTER 35

Declan received another phone call from the person at Udelhoven's real estate office the day after Joe's funeral. A priest from St. Mary's church had said the funeral mass. Hundreds of people attended. No one seemed to care, not even the priest, that Joe had committed suicide. Everyone was ready to forgive and to celebrate his life. Declan politely declined to do a reading or say any words at the service. He said that he could not do it.

The woman gave him directions to a small ravine in the country near the Placid development. She told him that she had placed some documents in a plastic bag and hid them under a rock in the ravine, and that he should wait until night when all of the workmen had left the area to retrieve the package. Declan thought that the informant had been reading too many crime novels and that her directions were a cloak-and-dagger cliché. But he was willing to play along because she seemed sincere and she was an insider who had solid information.

As Declan neared the Placid construction site, he could see dozens of homes in various stages of completion. He could already tell that they looked like houses from the English countryside. He turned down a rugged road. His car rattled as it passed over the frozen mud.

He looked at the directions that he had written down. Snow began to fall and the wind whipped the bare trees. He wanted to find the package before the weather turned worse.

He carefully walked down into a small gully that offered moderate protection from the wind. He could feel his face beginning to freeze. His nose began to run. He wiped it with the back of his glove.

He turned on his flashlight and began searching for the package. To his left, he noticed a large boulder with footprints near it. He walked over and picked up clear sandwich bag that had papers in it. It had been stuffed under the rock. As he began to open the bag, he heard a sharp crack against a nearby tree and felt splinters hit his jacket. He turned and crouched down as another shot whizzed by his head and into the frozen ground. He turned off his flashlight and began to run the length of the gully.

He couldn't see the person behind him but he could hear twigs cracking and footsteps hitting the ground. The cold air began to burn his nose and lungs as he continued up and out of the gully and into a large open area that was once a cornfield but that had been cleared for the Placid houses. Piles of wood and other building materials were scattered on the ground that was rapidly being covered by snow. He knew that he did not want to be out in the open. He also knew that his pursuer could track him easily in the snow.

In the distance were woods that sloped down to an abandoned quarry where he and Joe used to play as children. He ran as close as he could to the piles of wood and mounds of dirt that had been excavated for basements. Another shot slammed into one of these mounds as he passed behind it. He was only a few dozen yards from the woods now. He stuffed his package into his jacket.

As he entered the woods he tripped over a dead tree trunk and fell hard into the snow. He quickly looked back to see a figure walking swiftly toward him, holding a gun in his right hand.

Declan arose and hurried through the woods until he was at the precipice of the quarry wall. Beneath him were three terraces that led to the quarry floor about one hundred feet below him. He could feel that the footing on the rocks was icy. He had scrambled down these rock paths before, but in the summer when it was dry and there was light and he was an agile ten-year-old boy.

He began descending carefully down the rock path, intent on getting to the first terrace before his pursuer arrived. His muscles tensed as he put all of his energy into avoiding a fall. He made it to the first terrace and began running across the flat, open space to the edge where he would begin to make his way down to the second terrace. He didn't look back.

He gripped the edge of the second terrace and swung his legs down like he was descending a ladder. He heard a scream, the sound of rocks falling and then a hard thud. The person who had been chasing him had slipped and fallen down to the first terrace. The person swore and moaned and clutched his left shoulder and arm. Declan could not tell if the person still had the gun.

After a quick look, Declan continued down the slope to the next terrace and then to the third. After he finally reached the quarry floor, on which sat the rusting skeletons of cranes that had been used to move the heavy rock slabs, he ran toward the entry road that exited on Route 3, about a mile from where he had parked his car.

The snow was getting heavier and the air colder, and Declan's clothes were drenched in sweat. He saw a farmhouse about two hundred yards in the distance. He plodded through the snow along the shoulder of the road and then turned into the house's gravel driveway. He rang the doorbell. A man answered. Declan calmly introduced himself as a reporter for the *Lacroix Herald* and asked the stranger to call the police and an ambulance. Declan felt inside his jacket. The package had not fallen out.

CHAPTER 36

Ellen writhed underneath Alan. Her hands had been tied with silk scarves to his bedposts. Her legs rested on his shoulders as he thrust into her to the rapid tempo of Handel's *Music for the Royal Fireworks*. She pulled tight on the scarves as she and the music reached their respective climaxes.

After undoing her bonds, Alan rolled off of her and went to pour them each of glass of port. He looked outside. The snow storm was getting worse. Drifts began to form on his lawn and in the streets. They avoided talking about the fire Alan had set at Declan's. Ellen had other ways of showing her satisfaction with the fact that he had followed her instructions.

"I had a juicy conversation with Harry earlier tonight," Ellen said, preferring to share her joy in thrusting a knife into Harry.

"So you said. Do tell," Alan said, handing her a glass.

"Well, I received a charming little blackmail note this afternoon claiming that my dearly beloved was screwing a Mexican whore on a regular basis. The anonymous entrepreneur asked for twenty-five thousand dollars to keep the whole thing quiet and not cause me political embarrassment."

"So did our favorite foot doctor deny everything?"

"Actually, no. I must give him credit for unashamedly confirming that he has a wandering dick. He was quite calm and quite unapologetic. The bastard."

"Are you going to pay the blackmailer the money? Are you going to call the police? What?"

"Of course not, dear. In fact, I'm going to be the one who leaks Harry's indiscretion to the local newspaper. It will make him the pariah of the country club. And it won't do his practice any good either I'm thinking. In fact, this will be my excuse for filing for divorce and getting rid of him once and for all. I'll be the woman scorned. This is just the kind of sympathy I can capitalize on in my state senate bid. Harry did me a favor by going after some south-of-the-border pussy," Ellen explained.

"Do you think that Harry knows about us, and your other, shall I say, extra-marital detours?"

"I don't think he's that clever. But even if he suspected, he would never do anything. It helps his practice to be married to the mayor. Anyway, I'm going to launch a preemptive strike."

"And what does this mean for me?"

"It means the status quo until after the election in the fall. You know that. No time to get greedy now, Alan. Do you have any complaints about our arrangement? I didn't see you complaining a few minutes ago when your cock was getting some magnum opus cunt."

"No. No, I have no complaints, Ellen. I was just thinking of the conducting job at state college that you mentioned."

"Be patient and you'll get your post. Now lay back and assume the position," Ellen said as she climbed on top of Alan and began licking his chest and stomach. She decided then that she would need to cut herself loose of this second-rate maestro.

CHAPTER 37

The heavy snow buried any trace of the person who shot at Declan except for a glove that one of the officers found lodged between some rocks on the first terrace of the quarry.

"Whomever was chasing you didn't stay around even though he might have been injured, " Nora told Declan. After being shot at, Declan told Nora about his anonymous contact at the Placid Partnership. With the clues that the woman had given him about her prior relationship with Holstrom, Nora discovered that her name was Janet McDonough. She was Holstrom's ex-wife. Nora brought her in for questioning. She admitted placing the package in the gully, but she claimed that she was not setting Declan up. Nora believed her.

"She's trying to get back at her ex-husband, not kill you," Nora said.

"That's a comfort to know."

"She said that she didn't think she was being followed, but that's obviously not the case. Someone knew where she was going and was waiting for you," Nora said.

Declan and Nora examined the papers that Janet had provided. The materials showed evidence of payments to Carl Holstrom of over fifty-thousand dollars in the last two months for "special projects."

"Whatever these projects might have been, there's still no evidence to tie Holstrom to the murder of the Reynoldses. His alibi checks out. All these papers show is that he and George Udelhoven have an unusual business relationship," Nora said.

"Do we know where Holstrom was last night?"

"Yes, he was at the strip club Howl across the river. I've had him followed for the past several weeks. He wasn't the one who shot at you."

"But I still think he and Udelhoven are in on something."

"I do, too. I'm going to bring both of them in and try to play one off the other. We'll see if that gets us anywhere," Nora said.

"Pardon me for changing the subject from my near death experience, but what do you make of the mayor's announcement today?"

"It's got everyone talking, that's for sure."

"I would imagine. It's not every day that a mayor holds a press conference to announce that she and her husband are getting a divorce and that her husband's infidelity is the cause. "

"And you thought that coming back to Lacroix would be boring," Nora said, laughing. "Shame on you for having such low expectations for our fair little town."

"You know, ever since I've been back I've heard rumors about Ellen Norberg. My colleagues tell me that she has a history as well. But that no one can prove anything or is willing to admit to anything indiscreet."

"She's a woman. She's smarter and more discreet than most men, if the rumors are true that is. So do you think she's attractive? You've interviewed her."

"Of course. She oozes sex and political savvy. It's a man world, and she's not ashamed of taking advantage of any and all of her assets. I find that admirable. That's what makes her a successful politician. She going to play the wounded spouse all the way to the state house, and probably beyond."

"I don't know, but I find her too much like a female gladiator. Instead of a sword and armor she wields short dresses and cleavage."

"Those can be lethal weapons in the political arena."

"Spare me the tortured metaphor, Declan. I've got to go."

"How are things, Nora? I mean at home with Randy and the kids."

"Why do you want to know?"

FIRE AND ICE

"It's just that you don't see to talk about them more."

Nora paused and adjusted her sweater.

"Some days, Declan, I stare and stare at that French calendar you bought me and wish I could go there. I can smell the flowers and feel the sun on my neck. I wish I has the courage to go there years ago. But I was too timid. Too willing to settle for the known, the conventional, the secure rather than for the adventure. I feel that my mind just froze about fifteen years ago. Froze like a river in winter."

"Do you still love Randy?"

"That's not something I'm prepared to talk to you about, Declan."

"Not yet, or not ever?"

Nora didn't answer. She arose from the chair and went over to Declan to kiss him on the cheek.

"That's the only answer I can give you right now."

"I guess that will have to do."

"I guess it will. Can you stay for just a little longer? I'll play some Puccini for you."

"Only if it's *La Bohème*," Nora said.

"An excellent choice," Declan said.

CHAPTER 38

"I told you everything I know about that woman—Christa Bennington. We went through all of this before," Carl said as he tilted back in his chair in the police headquarters' interrogation room. "I got nothing more to say on the subject."

"Do you like to hunt, Carl? Maybe with a shotgun?" Nora said.

"Yeah, sometimes with my dad and with friends."

"We didn't find a shotgun at your new townhouse, Carl. Where do you keep it? You told me it was upstairs in this house."

"Oh yeah, I forgot. My girlfriend doesn't want guns in the house so I keep it at my friend Barry's place. He has a gun safe. I should have told you before. Go ahead and ask him."

"We're not going to find that you used it recently, are we, Carl?"

"Fuck no. Duck and pheasant season is over. You know that as well as I do. What are you getting at anyway?"

"Are we going to find that your gun was used to kill Judd and Miriam Reynolds? And that you did it for George Udelhoven? That he paid you to do it—fifty thousand dollars to be precise," Nora said.

"I don't know what you're talking about."

"We have the records, Carl. We have the records that show that George Udelhoven paid you fifty thousand dollars over the past few months. And that you then turned around and bought shares in the Placid Partnership for a steep discount. You're not that great of a carpenter, Carl," Nora said. "So the only thing I can conclude is that he paid you to kill them. Why? They wouldn't sell their property, is that it? He knew your history, your temper, and he paid you to get them out of the way so that he could negotiate with their son who was more willing to sell. That's how it happened, isn't it, Carl?"

Carl sat silently.

"Nothing to say, Carl? Fine. I hope you remember that you had your chance to talk when you're in prison for the rest of your life and George Udelhoven is making even more money than he does now," Nora said. "Let's go. I'm placing you under arrest for the murder of the Reynoldses."

"Wait. Just wait a fucking minute here."

"I'm tired of waiting, Carl. This better be good."

"OK. OK. Udelhoven did pay me that money. But it wasn't for carpentry work and it sure as hell wasn't for killing those farmers. I wouldn't do that," he said. "And I don't know nothing about who did. I swear to God."

"Carl, you're a real saint."

"Look, he paid me for getting him women, for himself and for potential investors in the Placid development. You know, women that would fuck him and those deep pockets guys from Chicago and Minneapolis."

"You're telling me that you ran a prostitution ring for the benefit of George Udelhoven?"

"Yeah. Me and my girlfriend Anna. You see, Anna's the one who met him first. He was one of her regulars. Then Anna and me approached him about getting other women to be available to help him with his business interests."

"You're a real savvy entrepreneur, Carl."

"Anyway, so you see, I had nothing to do with killing those people. All I know is that Udelhoven liked to fuck around, and I supplied him with the kind of women he liked, for a fee, of course."

"No wonder you could afford that new townhouse and the investment."

"Just because I'm not so well educated doesn't mean I'm not smart. That I don't have dreams. I do. So does Anna. We just went about getting things in a different way. We didn't hurt anybody. Everyone involved was a willing participant. It's strictly business, you know. So are you going to arrest me or what?

"You know, Carl, that would I guess be the proper thing to do. But I'm not going to do it. Let's keep the facts about your little business between us. I'm interested in solving a murder, not busting a prostitution ring. At least not right now. But remember that I know about it. And that I can call in my chips whenever I want to," Nora said. "And I swear to God that if you're story doesn't check out you'll wish you never met me."

"Sure, sure. I hear you detective. I'm telling you the truth. Anna and I want to keep our enterprise discreet. But on that murder thing, you need to talk to Udelhoven," Carl said.

"Why thank you, Carl, for that suggestion. I just might do that," Nora said. "Now get out of here."

Carl walked briskly out of the police station. He decided that he would keep the police interrogation to himself. There was no need to upset Anna. Better let sleeping whores lie, he said to himself, chuckling. He looked for a cigarette and then decided that he needed a beer and a shot of whiskey.

CHAPTER 39

Teresa had not attended mass with her mother for months. Maria was surprised that Teresa wanted to join her. As she sat in the pew, Teresa was not listening to the service or to the priest's sermon. She was engaged in her own private conversation with God. She asked forgiveness for her sins. She also tried to explain that what she was doing was for the benefit of her mother. She explained in her prayers that life is hard for poor people and that you have to make your own breaks to make your situation better. She and her mother worked very hard and had sacrificed, she explained, and now they were nearing their goal of buying a house and living a more secure life. She wished that she had been strong enough to avoid doing certain things, but not everyone can be a saint. She promised God, however, that she would make amends for her waywardness, that she would venture on a different path once her goal had been reached.

Maria looked at her daughter clutching her hands together and bowing her head. She smiled and touched Teresa hands, thinking that God had blessed her with a wonderful child who was always looking to make her life easier.

The night before, Teresa had been at Anna's house discussing what they would do now that Mayor Norberg had thwarted their blackmail plans by going public with her husband's indiscretions. Teresa complained that now she had lost a paying client whom she would have to replace. Anna told her that these downturns sometimes happen in the business world.

"I guess we underestimated the bitch, "Anna said. "How many politicians would have hung their spouse out to dry like that? She must have really hated the guy."

"Maybe we were being too greedy. We just didn't understand high-class people like the mayor," Teresa.

"People like her are just like you and me," Anna said. "Don't you forget it. They just have more money. But they aren't really different. If they were hungry and couldn't pay the bills, they'd be in the food lines at the church with the laid off factory workers. They just know how to play the game better, and they deal the cards. We just have to figure out how to get our hands on the card deck. But, hey, forget about our little scheme. She trumped us. Big fucking deal. We're still making good money."

"What does Carl think about this?"

"Carl doesn't know a damn thing. And don't you mention it to him either. It was our secret. Carl doesn't need to know what I'm doing every waking moment. You have to be independent. One day Carl and I will go our own separate ways. I've been keeping my own little cash stash as I call it, just in case. A woman has to be prepared. Someday I plan on opening up a chain of hair and nail salons. I'll join the chamber of commerce. Maybe I'll even buy myself a house out there in Placid. I kind of like those English manor houses that you see on public television. They're very refined. Do you know what I'm talking about?"

"Not really," Teresa said.

"Here, let me show you," Anna said. She pulled out a copy of a glossy four-color brochure about Thomas Conrad and the Placid development. "Take a look at this. It's beautiful, isn't it? That's why all of those people from the big cities are coming here, to live in a place like that. It would be nice to live in a place so serene, so cultured."

"This house is very beautiful," Teresa noted. "I hope my mother and I can find a place as nice. But I have to concentrate first on getting more clients."

"You will. No problem. I will help with that. That's what friends are for. But look at this house again. It's nice, but it's just the start. You are where you live, girl. You gotta dream big, and do what it takes to get there. You have to own your own life and not someone else own you. I know that you don't like doing some of the things you do. But, fuck, it ain't hurting anybody. And you enjoy it sometimes, you told me so. It's a stepping stone. The first rung on your career ladder. I read that in some magazine."

"Maybe you're right. I think about where I was a few months ago. I was bent over some stranger's toilet. I'm better than that."

"Now you're talking. Now let me tell you about this guy from the district attorney's office. He likes women who dress like nurses. Are you up for it? He pays double for the nurse thing."

"I can meet him tomorrow night. Go ahead and set it up," Teresa said. "Can I borrow this brochure? I'd like to read more about this place called Placid."

"Go ahead. Maybe some day we'll be neighbors, talking to each other across our white picket fence while we tend to our roses," Anna said. "Now wouldn't that be a fucking hoot."

CHAPTER 40

Declan could not believe that his brother-in-law Tommy was cooking steaks on his grill in the middle of February. But warm winds from the west had driven the temperature into the sixties, even though there was still over a foot of snow on the ground. While Declan, his sister Moira and Tommy sipped beers on the deck, Moira's children made snowmen in the backyard.

"This has really been a weird winter," Tommy said while turning over the steaks.

"You mean you don't wear short sleeves and grill steaks every February?" Declan said. His sister had invited him over to take advantage of the winter warmth but also to talk to him about what every one in Lacroix was talking about: the arrest of George Udelhoven for the murder of Judd and Miriam Reynolds.

"So Declan, give us the real scoop," Moira said. "If I'm going to have a brother who's a newspaper editor, I want to know all of the sordid details, even those that didn't make it into print."

"Yeah, Declan, spill the beans," Tommy chimed in.

"I thought you two adults read our fine local newspaper," Declan said. He had never told his sister about being attacked in the quarry. The attacker had been George Udelhoven.

"The truth is that Nora Morrissey and I had been gathering evidence for a while that always seemed to point in the direction of his company," Declan continued. "But at first we thought it was someone who worked for Udelhoven."

"Who?"

"I can't say, Moira. I don't want to say anything about an innocent man. Let's just say that we were on the wrong track for a while. Eventually, the evidence led to Udelhoven. He had the shotgun. He had been fighting with the Reynoldses for months trying to buy their land. He even tried to bribe their children into helping him win over the Reynoldses. But nothing seemed to work. I guess there was too much at stake in the whole Placid development, and he just snapped. He's claiming that the gun shot was an accident."

"But setting a fire was no accident," Moira said.

"You are right about that," Declan said. "We'll see what a jury decides. Udelhoven has hired some high-flying lawyer from Chicago. He figures this guy will dazzle the local yokels here in Lacroix. And now the district attorney is looking into the finances of the Placid Partnership. Mayor Norberg and Thomas Conrad are taking the lead in trying to keep the whole development going. There's a lot of money and jobs and prestige at stake here."

"Something tells me that they'll succeed. People like them usually do, Tommy said.

"I just can't believe that somebody like George Udelhoven could do such a grisly thing. He was so ordinary," Moira said.

"I think that's exactly why he did it. He wanted to be more than just common and conventional. He perversely saw Judd Reynolds as a roadblock to his grand vision. People do strange things for money," Declan said.

"All these things happening in our town—murders, suicides, big money investments. Lacroix was once an anonymous, quiet place to live," Moira said.

"Ellen Norberg is betting that people still think it is all of those quaint things," Declan said. "She has some grand ambitions. She'll end up in the state capital one day. Either that or prison. It's an even bet one way or the other now I think."

"I don't want to talk stuff like that on a glorious day like this. So tell me, Declan, you seem to spend a lot of time with Nora. Anything to tell?" Moira said.

"Melville and I get along fine. And Nora is still married," Declan said.

"I always thought her husband Randy was the human

equivalent of watching wet paint dry," Moira said. "You and Nora should have got married a long time ago."

"Yes, what might have been. But Randy and Nora have two children. So let's respect that, shall we."

"But you can dream, can't you?"

"Maybe that's why I have my books, my music and my travels."

"Fine. I was just asking. I'll butt out."

"Thank you."

"Steaks are up everybody, " Tommy said. "Grab a plate and dig in. We're never going to see a day like this until May."

"Yes, it's better than Christmas," Declan muttered as he walked to the grill.

CHAPTER 41

Nora watched her daughters Alexandra and Jenna splash in the pool under the warm spring sun in Provence. Shimmering in the distance were rocky, lavender hills, beneath which sat the small French village with red-tiled roofs where Nora and the girls would drive each day for fresh bread and vegetables. It was late morning in March, and the blue sky glistened like the edge of a knife. Afternoon thunderstorms would make the skies frown. Whatever the weather, Nora relished the smells and the sounds and the vistas of the place about which she had dreamed for so long. The contrast with Lacroix stunned her each morning she awoke.

After George Udelhoven was arrested for killing the Reynoldses, Nora asked for a leave of absence from the police force. She asked Randy if he wanted to join her in France for a few weeks. Most of their previous vacations had been to his family's cabin in Minnesota. Randy declined, citing business considerations at the car dealership and his routine of traveling to one or more venues of the NCAA basketball tournament with friends from high school. He told her that it was a tradition that he did not want to miss. So Nora came to France with the girls.

Declan had helped her search for a rental home and loaned her his French language books and tapes. She considered it a small victory when she learned all the words for the daily grocery list. She and her daughters spent their days in the pool or taking walks through the hills or just reading on the patio. She was surprised that neither Alexandra nor Jenna fussed too much about missing television or videos. She was proud of their willingness to adapt, if only for a few weeks.

She sat down in a chair by the pool and poured herself a glass of lemonade. The cold ice sparked in the sun. A warm breeze crept up from the valley.

She began to write a letter to Declan. She told him that it was wonderful to be away from the cold and the grays and browns of winter. She told him that it was good to be away from death and betrayal. She told him that she wished that he could have joined her because she knew how much he adored France. She told him that she always admired his adventurous spirit. She told him that it was difficult to undo the choices one made in the past. Finally, she told him that she was not certain where her life would lead her, but that the time in France had been a portal to new possibilities for her.

She looked at her daughters and could see Randy. She looked across the fields in the distance and could see Declan. She wondered where she would have to gaze to see herself.

The End

ABOUT THE AUTHOR

William Graham is a graduate of Northwestern University. He and his wife Jacqueline live in Chicago, Illinois, with their son Jack.